REIGN
of OUTLAWS

Also by Kekla Magoon

Shadows of Sherwood
Rebellion of Thieves

REIGN of OUTLAWS

A ROBYN HOODLUM ADVENTURE

KEKLA MAGOON

BLOOMSBURY

NEW YORK   LONDON   OXFORD   NEW DELHI   SYDNEY

First published in the United States of America in October 2017
by Bloomsbury Children's Books
www.bloomsbury.com

Bloomsbury is a registered trademark of Bloomsbury Publishing Plc

For information about permission to reproduce selections from this book, write to
Permissions, Bloomsbury Children's Books, 1385 Broadway, New York, New York 10018
Bloomsbury books may be purchased for business or promotional use. For information on
bulk purchases please contact Macmillan Corporate and Premium Sales Department at
specialmarkets@macmillan.com

Library of Congress Cataloging-in-Publication Data
Names: Magoon, Kekla, author.
Title: Reign of outlaws / by Kekla Magoon.
Description: New York : Bloomsbury, 2017.
Summary: Twelve-year-old Robyn Loxley has seventy-two hours to decide between sacrificing
herself to save her parents and friends, or continuing to lead the rebellion to rid Nott City
of Ignomus Crown once and for all.
Identifiers: LCCN 2017016402 (print) • LCCN 2017035048 (e-book)
ISBN 978-1-61963-657-6 (hardcover) • ISBN 978-1-61963-658-3 (e-book)
Subjects: | CYAC: Robbers and outlaws—Fiction. | Adventure and adventurers—Fiction. |
Government, Resistance to—Fiction. | Rescues—Fiction.
Classification: LCC PZ7.M2739 Rei 2017 | (print) LCC PZ7.M2739 (e-book)
DDC [Fic]—dc23
LC record available at https://lccn.loc.gov/2017016402

Book design by Amanda Bartlett and John Candell
Typeset by Westchester Publishing Services
Printed and bound in the U.S.A. by Berryville Graphics Inc., Berryville, Virginia
2 4 6 8 10 9 7 5 3 1

All papers used by Bloomsbury Publishing, Inc., are natural, recyclable products
made from wood grown in well-managed forests. The manufacturing processes
conform to the environmental regulations of the country of origin.

For Alice, Iris, Liam, and Will

≪CHAPTER ONE≫

The Fire

A fire blazed in the heart of Sherwood County, in the heart of Tent City, in the heart of a single girl.

Robyn Loxley gazed into the flames. Their heat lapped her face, a welcome contrast to the cool morning air. The red tongues danced upward, fierce and unending. Untouchable.

She knew she should leave. It wasn't safe to be out in the open. There was a price on her head, and the Military Police patrolling the area would not hesitate to take her into custody. Or worse.

But still she stood there.

This fire, in this spot, had burned for hundreds of years. Maybe longer. In the moon lore prophecy, the fire represented the center of things, a place from which life sprang, and a place to which life returned. A union of Shadows and Light.

She should leave, and quickly. But the fire drew her closer. If she could truly take it into herself, truly become like the flames, she would understand what needed to be done.

Standing here, in the warmth, all things felt possible. To save her parents. To help Sherwood. To rid Nott City of Governor Crown once and for all.

A gentle wind blew, and the flames nipped higher. As if they could hear her thoughts.

As soon as she stepped away, things would become harder again. She knew it.

Robyn fingered the scrap of silver cloth in her hand. Another puzzle to solve. Part of the moon lore? There were more questions than answers in the world, it seemed. She fought the sudden urge to toss the cloth into the flames, never to know its mysteries. Never to have to try.

Robyn's throat tightened. It would be easy to get stuck thinking about all the things she had lost.

Her attempt to rescue her mother had gone awry.

Her friends Laurel and Tucker had sacrificed themselves so that Robyn could get away.

Sheriff Mallet had stolen her pendant, a gift from her parents and the key to the moon shrine, Robyn's private refuge.

And worst of all—

The heavy sound of boots on pavement startled Robyn out of her spiraling thoughts.

She forced herself away from the fire circle. She strode determinedly through the cardboard shelters, her ears perked for the sound of MPs. They would not take her down. Not today.

Not ever.

The moon lore spoke of a child who could be as the fire. Occasionally, for a second, Robyn could almost believe it was true of her. Most of the time it felt too big a task to fall to her alone.

"I'm not alone," she whispered. But it didn't feel true.

It had been hard enough to believe in these new friends in the first place. And now they had lied. Key and Scarlet had been plotting with Chazz behind her back the whole time. Chazz, who didn't like or trust Robyn, and kept trying to send her away altogether. They'd kept Robyn in the dark about their real plans. The rebellion was already much bigger than she realized. But they'd let her believe she was important.

Robyn eased her way around each cardboard wall, trying not to let her racing thoughts distract her from avoiding the MPs. All this time, she had been trying to help her parents, and it wasn't only for selfish reasons. She thought they needed her parents to get the rebellion back on track. She'd been trying to do something, trying to understand the new world she'd been thrust into. And instead of giving her the real answers, her so-called friends had let her make a fool of herself.

Who was she kidding? How had she believed that her silly Hoodlum antics could really make a difference to Sherwood?

When she reached the edge of the tents, Robyn looked both ways. This was the most exposed part of the walk. A long expanse of pavement with nothing to hide behind except the two tall stone pillars that marked the fairground entrance.

Robyn marched through the fairground gates, unsure where she was headed.

Her friends had lied to her. She had turned her back on them and run.

It was okay, though. Alone was better.

Alone was her way.

Running was also her way, sometimes. To escape seemed only logical, when the whole world was closing in.

The note her father had left her along with the keys to his old moped suggested she run far and fast. Get out of Nott City. Maybe it was time to do that.

It was close to dawn. Not close enough to lighten the sky, but close enough that the first wave of workers was headed to the borders. Most of the working-class men and women of Sherwood crossed the county line into neighboring Block Six each morning. The quarries, factories, lumberyards, and industrial complexes centered there employed thousands.

"Employed" was becoming a stretch, under Governor Crown's rule. Hours were longer, wages lower, and fists tightened all around. The changes had been gradual but significant over the past few months.

Everything was getting harder for the people of Sherwood. But that would change if the rebellion had anything to say about it.

Robyn pushed the thoughts aside.

A few days ago it had felt like they could take on anything, together. Now she knew the others didn't really want or need her. They had only let her believe she was a leader, while they worked behind her back the whole time. The betrayal stung.

Key, Chazz, and Scarlet could have their big rebellion. Obviously they didn't need her. Probably they were all still at the tree house, where she'd left them, planning things without her. Robyn was best on her own, anyway. How had she managed to lose sight of that?

A static squawk echoed overhead. The loudspeakers mounted high on lampposts around the neighborhood prepared to broadcast.

"Good morning, residents of Sherwood." Governor Crown's cold, pinched voice came through the air, sending shivers down Robyn's spine.

"This is a message to the hoodlum known as Robyn. We know who you are. We know what you were looking for when you came by tonight. Turn yourself in or it will be destroyed."

Crown was threatening her parents!

Robyn raged. Her heart burned with fresh fire.

It? How dare he call her mother *it?*

"You have seventy-two hours," Crown concluded. As the broadcast cut off, the city clock tower chimed. It was six a.m.

If Crown expected Robyn to deliver herself to his doorstep, ever, he had another thing coming.

Her hands closed into fists. Something soft in her right hand . . . oh. The section of cloth from Floyd Bridger.

Robyn tucked the silver scrap into her pocket. The fabric was just like the curtain in the moon shrine. In the moonlight, it might carry a message.

Perhaps she should have thrown this new scrap into the flames after all. The first moon lore message had led Robyn toward friends in the first place.

With their help, she had become the famous outlaw, the one they called "Robyn Hoodlum" on the wanted posters.

But she didn't need anyone else. Not anymore.

She could cause plenty of trouble for Crown on her own.

The thought surprised her. A minute ago she'd been ready to give up, to run away, leave the rebellion to the others. But in her heart, she realized that wasn't possible.

No matter how bad it felt, she couldn't give up on the cause. Her parents, now in prison, had given everything to make a difference. Robyn could, too.

≪CHAPTER TWO≫

Sacrifice

The three women clustered together, with their arms around one another. The girl stood defiantly apart. Her gaze raked across every inch of the stone walls, in search of a crack or crevice.

There was none.

Her small fists bound up and released, like a slow pulse.

Mrs. Loxley studied the young girl. The one whose death-defying leap onto the windshield of a moving vehicle had very likely spared her daughter's life. She couldn't have been more than nine or ten.

"There's too much bleeding," the youngest woman said.

Mrs. Loxley turned back to her friends. "Keep pressure on it," she told Verilyn.

The third woman had grown pale with blood loss from the gunshot to the side of her abdomen. "Hang in there, Susan." Mrs. Loxley took her hand. Susan was barely conscious. The ragged cloth of her nightdress was soaked through.

It was hard to believe what was happening. An hour ago, the three women had been locked in a dungeon prison cell, together with about a dozen others. They'd been hungry, cold, unsettled, and vaguely ill from months spent in the dark and the damp. Some too weak to move. Most too weary to speak. All clinging to their last shreds of strength just to keep breathing.

Then a light shone down the corridor. The women had tensed, awaiting the guards. Usually the light meant there would be trays with their meager allotment of food. Occasionally it meant someone would be taken. Questioned. Punished.

Instead, the group that rushed into their enclosure was young and wide-eyed. A group of children, led by Mrs. Loxley's daughter, Robyn.

How had they found the dungeon? How had they broken through Crown's defenses and gotten into the governor's mansion? There hadn't been time to find out. Everything had happened too quickly.

Robyn and her friends had rushed the women out of the prison cells. Mother and daughter had managed a quick embrace but not nearly long enough. Time was of the essence. Mrs. Loxley hadn't recognized any of the other children in the group, except for Governor Crown's niece, Merryan.

The escape plan almost worked.

Robyn had gotten behind the wheel of a van and driven off into the night. Mrs. Loxley sighed. Her twelve-year-old, driving? Her twelve-year-old *knew how* to drive? Robyn had always been precocious and would have loved to get behind the wheel from the time she was a toddler. But it terrified her mother to think that she'd been pressed into doing something so drastic. The best time to learn how to drive was NOT in the middle of a dangerous escape. She couldn't stop picturing Robyn in that van, careening in a high-speed chase away from Crown's guards.

Mrs. Loxley shook her head, trying to clear her thoughts. The pain of re-imprisonment was nothing. Not compared to the pain of wondering how it had turned out for Robyn. Was she okay?

She forced her attention away from what had happened earlier. Time to focus on what was happening here and now.

Mrs. Loxley moved toward the girl. Her large brown eyes would not stop moving.

"You were very brave," Mrs. Loxley said. "What you did allowed the others to escape."

The child was skittish as a cornered animal. Understandably so.

She inched a bit closer. "What's your name?"

The tiny girl stood stoic.

"You must be very good friends with my daughter."

A long while passed, in stillness and silence.

"You're Robyn's mom?" she said finally.

"Yes," Mrs. Loxley said. She tucked a strand of wild blond hair behind the girl's ear. As her thumb brushed over the girl's temple, the girl flinched.

"Oh, my dear." Mrs. Loxley drew her hand back. Maternal instincts cried for her to clutch the girl close, to comfort away the terror in her eyes. Instead she folded her hands against her stomach. "I'm so sorry."

The still-nameless girl studied Mrs. Loxley in return. She was clearly now an object of curiosity in the child's mind.

Susan's soft moans punctured the quiet.

"She's not going to make it," Verilyn whispered. "Not without real treatment."

Mrs. Loxley turned back to the other women. It was probably true. If the guards came soon, they could appeal to them for help. Although, they had nothing to offer in exchange, apart from continued obedience.

Obedience and . . . Mrs. Loxley stifled a gasp.

"Sweetheart," she said, grasping the child's shoulders. The girl tensed up instantly, but the time for gentle patience had passed. "Do you have information? Anything that the guards might want to know?"

The girl's large eyes grew even wider.

"You do, then," Mrs. Loxley murmured. "Will they know this?"

The girl dipped her pointed chin twice. She squirmed out of Mrs. Loxley's grasp.

"Oh, my dear."

The girl spoke for the second time. "What will they do?"

The women glanced at each other. Verilyn spoke. "They will want to question you," she said evenly.

Everyone in the room knew what that meant. The girl, however young, was not so innocent to the ways of the world. Mrs. Loxley ached at that.

"You should tell us what you know. Let them take us instead," Verilyn said.

The child's chin went up. "Don't worry. I won't tell them anything."

"They may not give you a choice."

The girl glanced from corner to corner around the small stone cell. "They could be listening."

That was true enough, but Mrs. Loxley doubted it. The jailbreak attempt had put the guards on the defensive. More likely, they were out there scrambling to regroup. Giving chase to those who had gotten further in the escape.

"You're the first person from the outside we've gotten to speak to in months. Other than the guards in the dungeon who brought in our food."

"Tell us something of the world," Verilyn added. "It's impossible, not knowing."

"But you already know, don't you?" the girl whispered. "For Sherwood, unite."

"For Sherwood, we fight," Mrs. Loxley finished.

"The rebellion is resurfacing?" Verilyn's voice held the hope they all longed for. "The people are gathering to fight?"

The girl nodded. "And Robyn is in charge."

Mrs. Loxley's heart fluttered. So it had been told. So it had been written. Still it was hard to believe that such legends would ever come to pass. That her baby girl would be tasked with . . .

Voices erupted outside the door, accompanied by the sound of keys clanging and chains dragging. A mess of sounds, unpleasant.

The women tightened their cluster. "Get behind us," Mrs. Loxley whispered urgently. But instead the girl leaped toward the door, pressed her body against the wall beside the doorknob, like a shadow.

The metal slab of a door burst open. A burly guard stepped through. He had to duck to pass into the enclosed space, and once he did, his looming presence dominated the room. A second guard ducked in after him.

Slippery as a moonbeam, the girl sprang into action. She darted between the guards and dodged around their legs, faster than they could even react.

The rear guard turned to chase the girl, but she was a streak of light.

Mrs. Loxley jumped up and ran around the front guard and out the door, too, giving the rear guard no choice but to subdue her instead of giving chase.

Mrs. Loxley smiled as they crashed to the ground. Her whole body ached, and she would no doubt suffer for this moment of defiance. But she could see over his shoulder. They were no longer in the bowels of the castle. This cell opened to the outside yards. Outside the door was a brief pool of torchlight. Beyond that, only darkness. The girl disappeared into the night.

⪡CHAPTER THREE⪢

Ready

Key left the tree house at first light. He wound his way through the trees toward Tent City. He stomped along, releasing his frustration on every stick lying in his path. The cracking sound they made satisfied something deep within him. Stomp. *Crack.* Stomp. *Crack.*

Chazz was making a mess out of everything. He was old. He sometimes couldn't see how the world had changed. He had led the Crescent Rebellion to success a generation ago, but that was then. This was now.

Chazz wanted to operate within a cloak of secrecy. But Key hated secrets. Secrets led to pain and misunderstanding.

Can't force it. She'll lead when she's ready. Till then, we work and we wait, Chazz kept saying.

Yes, Robyn was reckless. Key had known this all along. From the moment he had first run into her, it was clear she would take any bull by the horns. She wasn't afraid of anything. It amazed him.

Robyn liked to leap. Key held on to her shirttail and made her look first. There were reasons they worked well as a team. He hated to admit it, because at the moment he was just angry at her. For not trusting him. For running away.

He was mad at himself, too. He should have told Robyn the truth, if no one else was going to. Just like everyone should have told him the truth about his own life. Key knew how it felt to be misled. To be lied to.

Never a good idea to tell someone what they're not ready to hear. Chazz's words floated back to him. Along with the pointed expression he had worn. Key didn't believe in secrets. Some knowledge was too powerful to be locked away.

Chazz was wrong to think Robyn would magically pull it all together and take charge. She needed more information, more help. Key was the planner, the organizer, the one who thought things through.

He couldn't blame her for being mad, but was she really surprised? What did she think was going on? You couldn't run a rebellion on the back of a postage stamp. Right now they were a bunch of misfit kids, driven by impulse. It would need to be a well-oiled machine that took Crown down.

Crown.

Key clenched his fists. Thinking about the man in the tower always brought him to rage. Crown was selfish. Power hungry. Cruel. He cast people aside as useless. People who mattered. People who he should have— *No. Don't think about it*, Key reminded himself.

One thing Key had decided long ago: he would never be like Ignomus Crown.

Crown might cast people aside when they annoyed him, but Key would not do the same to Robyn.

She mattered. And they had been through too much already. No one got to walk away. Not him. Not Chazz. Not Robyn.

Key snuck through the patrol at the edge of the forest, much the way Robyn had several hours earlier. He thought he would find her at the fire, but the space was empty. Quiet, but for the soft lick of flames.

A blip of fear pulsed through him. If she wasn't here, where was she?

He rushed toward Nottingham Cathedral. What if he had waited too long to follow her? What if she had run? In the time he needed to think things through, Robyn could have made a half-dozen moves. Key was a ponderous chess game. Robyn was more like a blazing hot potato, always on the move.

The rebellion needed Robyn.

She knew how to get people excited, how to make them believe in something. She was a flame from which it was impossible to look away.

≪CHAPTER FOUR≫

Promises, Promises

"You have failed me."

"Sir—"

"I don't want to hear it, Sheriff." Governor Ignomus Crown stood perfectly still behind his desk. When he was motionless like that, it usually meant he was thinking, or else that he was angry to a place beyond words.

Sheriff Marissa Mallet forced herself to hold back the words that would have come next. She was angry, too. Mostly with the way Crown was acting like everything was her fault.

The hoodlum Robyn had infiltrated the Iron Teen contest. Mallet, of course, knew much more about the situation than she let on. It was bad enough to look like a failure. Crown wouldn't be able to appreciate the nuances of her choice to leave him in the dark. Her choice to let Robyn compete. To hide her real identity from Crown. These things might look like something worse than failure. Betrayal. Treason.

Mallet shifted uncomfortably in place. *It takes one to know one.* She wasn't the real traitor here. Not by a long shot.

Crown paced along behind his desk. Mallet hovered patiently near the wingback chairs on the other side. She wasn't going to sit. She could not appear to defer.

She dared not stand too close, though, either. It tended to remind him of her height advantage, and he had always been a small man who wanted to be the largest.

His stature may not have conveyed power, but his manner did.

The way he smoothed his thumb and index finger over his mustache, around his mouth. It drew her attention to his lips, to whatever he was about to say.

He made her wait for it.

She gritted her teeth and stood patiently.

The jerk.

She had been prepared to give him everything. Her loyalty. Her brilliance. Her energy. Her heart.

"Well, Marissa."

He called her by her first name. He did it now to bring her down, she knew. How well she knew. His mind, his games.

The door opened behind her. Mallet knew without looking, it would be Nick Shiffley, Governor Crown's chief of staff and de facto head of security. She could practically smell him coming. His particular aura of greed and cunning wafted off him like cologne.

The security job was rightfully hers. Shiffley hadn't earned his place at the top. He had weaseled his way in. She had put in the time. She had the experience. Shiffley was a politician, shrewd and oily. He knew how to make things look good. Mallet knew how to get things done. When was Crown going to realize he was ignoring one of his greatest assets?

When was he going to hand her the promotion he had assured her was coming? Police Commissioner of Nott City, the position Crown himself had held prior to his takeover. A takeover which, she could have pointed out, she and her officers had single-handedly facilitated.

Without her, Crown was nothing.

"I could be of help in securing this building," she said, glancing toward Shiffley. "And securing the entire city."

Shiffley's eyes narrowed. He understood. He, too, had failed last night.

"Get your own house in order, Sheriff," Shiffley said snidely. "And then we'll talk again."

The pesky hoodlum had a way of getting under everyone's skin. Crown's. Shiffley's. Mallet's. Robyn was a Sherwood problem, now gone to the Castle. A blip on Mallet's otherwise perfect service record.

"My business is with . . . the governor," Sheriff Mallet spoke coldly, kicking herself for chickening out on using his first name as he'd just done to her. Ignomus wouldn't look kindly on that, but it was no better than he deserved.

Securing one building was nothing compared to the work of securing an entire county. And Shiffley couldn't even manage that simple task. Her own job was much bigger. So she hadn't caught the hoodlum yet. True, but that was just one mistake in a landscape of greater successes. Including everything it had taken to put Crown in power.

"I think we're finished here, Sheriff."

Mallet's eyes narrowed. Crown had made promises to her. Promises that weren't contingent on performance, only loyalty. Her performance had been above board. Her loyalty, unwavering. Despite his repeated dismissals and betrayals. She had kept true to her word. If Crown wasn't prepared to do the same, it was time *he* started worrying.

Perhaps it was time to take a page from the hoodlum's playbook, and show Crown what she was truly capable of. There were consequences to underestimating her. She would catch Robyn. Catch her, but not for Crown.

"Very well." Mallet spun toward the door and strode out of the office. She resisted the instinct to look over her shoulder. Crown would not see her beg for his attention. Not anytime soon.

Without her, he was nothing. It was time he realized it.

≪CHAPTER FIVE≫

Seventy-Two Hours

It didn't take Robyn long to gather all her stuff. A few changes of clothes and some thieving gear, her moped keys, her TexTer.

Robyn stalked through the rooms of the crumbling Nottingham Cathedral. The bedroom they shared with its mattresses on the floor. The kitchen, with its few remaining provisions. The space with Scarlet's security setup. The office with its wide wooden desk and ratty orange sofa.

She laid her TexTer on the desk. Maybe the others could use it.

Time to go.

There was no one to stop her, no one to ask questions. It would be the easiest thing in the world to slip out the door, pull her moped from its hiding place, and disappear.

And go where? They'd know to look for her at the tree house. She'd have to improvise until she figured something out. Seventy-two hours. She could make do until then. She'd figure out her plan, and she'd save them. And then it would all be over.

A vision of home surrounded her. Her canopy bed, her playroom, the moon porch where she could see the sky. The kitchen, full of music and smelling like Dad's latest attempt at dinner. The kitchen floor, dripping with blood.

No. Robyn shook her head, sinking back into the fantasy. The gardens Mom tended. Art on the walls. The shed, where she and Dad used to tinker. The live oak in the backyard that she loved to climb . . .

Leaves rustled behind her. Robyn's heart pounded. She spun around and came face to face with . . . Governor Crown! The scream tore upward from the base of her belly. Clawlike hands reached out toward her and—

Robyn woke with a start. The vision of trees and grasping claws in front of her gave way to the dim, cool interior room. A crumbling wall of jagged brown bricks.

Her cheeks were damp, her body cramped and awkward, curled on the hard orange sofa. She raised her neck off the threadbare arm, immediately aware of stiffness in her muscles.

These surroundings were a far cry from the pristine face of Loxley Manor. Robyn stretched and flexed her limbs as recognition of her real life trickled back in, pressing the dream toward the recesses of her mind, where it belonged.

Robyn wished it had been only a dream, not partly a memory. She wanted to forget finding her parents' blood in the kitchen, believing they'd been killed by Governor Crown's newly formed Military Police forces, fleeing through the trees to get to safety—that part was all real. All too real, even though several months had passed, and she now knew her parents were alive.

At least for now.

Robyn pulled off her left glove—the one she constantly wore, even while sleeping—and gazed at the back of her hand. At the Tag emblazoned there in bold black tattoo ink. Her only remaining connection to—

"Oh, thank the moon." Key burst into the room, ducking under the broken wall and picking his way through the rubble.

Robyn hastily replaced her glove. Instinct.

Key saw her do it, but made no comment. Robyn glanced away from him. More than once, she had trusted Key with her life. But not her secrets.

Perhaps they didn't really know each other at all.

Key perched his short, lanky frame on the opposite sofa arm, breathing hard, saying nothing. Robyn snapped her glove in place across her wrist. The tiny metal click seemed deafening. She met Key's gaze and held it, unsure whether to apologize, or wait for him to, or let it all be water under the bridge.

She had meant to be gone before they got back. To avoid this awkward moment.

She had yelled. She had run away from everyone. But Key had lied. Beneath her sleepy sadness, rumblings of his betrayal still churned in her gut.

Key scratched his temple, flicking aside unruly locks of blond hair, as he gazed down at Robyn. He lowered his arm, glancing at the dark rectangle tattooed on the back of his own hand. Perhaps to remind her that she didn't know his number, either. He'd had it blacked out in protest.

Robyn swung her legs aside to make room for Key's feet on the cushion. "Why am I sleeping on the couch?" She didn't know how to say what was really on her mind.

Key shrugged. "It's been a long night."

"Yeah." Robyn rolled her shoulders. Was it just going to be like this? They were never going to speak of what had happened? Did he think things could just go back to normal?

Key pressed his hand against his chest and bent forward. He looked all clammy and red in the face. Robyn gazed at him skeptically. "Are you okay?"

He nodded. "I just"—he breathed—"ran really hard. My heart is pounding."

"Do you even have a heart?" Robyn snapped. The moment of concern gave way to her annoyance and anger.

"If not, I come by it honestly," Key retorted.

"What is that supposed to mean?" Robyn said, planting her fists on her knees.

Key glared. "You don't know everything. About anything. Stop acting like the whole world should cater to you."

"Not the whole world," Robyn blurted out. "Just my so-called friends."

They were both looking at Robyn's packed bag, on the floor at her feet. It seemed to prove Key's point.

"I'm sorry, okay?" Key said finally. "Chazz said you'd freak out if you knew everything."

Robyn scoffed. "Who cares what Chazz thinks?"

Key looked surprised. "Kind of . . . everyone?"

Robyn stood up. She rolled her aching shoulders and shot him a dirty look. She tried to find the normal, joking tone they usually shared. "We need an interior decorator around here. This couch is not okay." Her usual mattress wasn't exactly a palace luxury item, but at least it didn't leave her joints feeling all kinky and unoiled. "New house rule: If you ever catch me snoozing here again, you better wake me."

Key grinned, leaping off the couch and moving toward the gap in the wall that used to be a doorway. "Easy for you to say. You don't have to deal with sleepy-bear you."

"What are you trying to say?" Robyn planted her fists on her hips and glared, jokingly this time.

"I have strong self-preservation instincts," Key quipped, looking back. "They tell me not to interrupt your REM cycle, on pain of suffering and possibly death."

Robyn rolled her eyes. "Gee, don't hold back," she drawled. Not that she could deny she got grumpy when overtired.

And she was tired. Still. She sat back down on the couch and rubbed her eyes with the heels of her hands. Her eyelashes clumped wetly against her skin. She swiped at her cheeks and let her face rest in her hands a moment.

"You wanna talk about anything?" The words slipped out of Key, all quiet.

Robyn glanced his way, surprised he was still in the room. "Weird dream," she mumbled. "That's all."

Quiet settled over them, sure as the stones. Key lowered himself onto the half wall of broken rock and gazed at her in that way of his. The way that said he knew her truth already, despite the things that had never been said between them.

There were things she could say. The words rose up and threatened to choke her. But they wouldn't come out. Too much had happened. Too much . . . could still happen.

"Seventy-two hours," she said finally. And maybe that was enough.

"What?" Key said.

Oh. Right. Key had just come out of the woods, the only place where there were no speakers. The only place safe from Crown's reach, from Crown's voice.

It was hard to say the thing out loud. "Crown knows who I am. He set a new deadline. My parents die in seventy-two hours. Unless I turn myself in."

"We'll think of something," Key said.

Robyn stared dejectedly at a boarded-up window. "Or, we already blew it. We messed up our one chance to save at least my mom." Her chest tightened up with regret. The scene in the governor's mansion gardens played out over and over in her mind. Mom throwing herself on a guard so the others could escape.

"I don't know," Key said. "But, let's get to work."

Key disappeared through the gap in the wall. Heading out the opposite way, Robyn went to the bedroom. Her mattress was the one nearest the door—this room still actually had a door, which is why they'd chosen it for their sleep space—so all she had to do was stick her arm into the room to deposit the bag she'd packed. She returned her toothbrush to the plastic cup beside her mattress. Lifelong habits die hard. It was funny, her whole life she'd resisted small chores. Making the bed. Brushing her teeth. Now she clung to the tiny routines. The hints of normalcy. Dull tasks like doing the dishes took on new meaning when any meal could not be taken for granted.

She picked her way through the rubble to the bathroom sink. The water ran cold.

They were out of toothpaste. She added it to her mental shopping list, somewhere near the bottom. Food was more important. Anyway Laurel would take care of . . .

Laurel.

Robyn's chest twisted into itself.

Laurel, splayed across the jeep windshield like a starfish, blocking the MPs' advance.

How could Robyn even think about leaving, with Laurel in trouble? Laurel, who'd sacrificed herself to save Robyn and the others.

The gnawing in her stomach could no longer be ignored. Robyn headed into the kitchen. On the wooden plank that served as their dinner table sat two bread heels in a plastic bag.

Robyn took one and filled a cup with water. She slipped through another wall—the wall she figured had once held the room's actual door—and into the hallway. From the next room came the familiar click-clicking of Scarlet's servers, constantly checking and re-checking the various digital protections that kept their hideout carefully shrouded from the everywhere eyes of the Nott City Military Police. Robyn shuddered slightly. She glanced in the computer room, but saw no sign of Scarlet. Just the row of flat, blinking machines and their steady, clicking hum. Among other things, Scarlet's interface kept all the nearby public surveillance cameras running on a twenty-four-hour loop in which nothing at all happened, so the four of them could come and go as they pleased without drawing attention.

Key came down the hall carrying two full loaves of bread.

"Where'd you get that?"

"I bartered," he said. "Cost me the last of our fresh oranges. Yesterday, before—"

A loud boom echoed, drowning out his voice. It sounded like ten claps of thunder rippling right through the room.

"What the—?" Robyn leaped toward the boarded-up window and peered through the cracks. She couldn't see anything but the concrete slab wall of the building across the alley.

"They're building the barricade," Key said, calmly taking a sip of water. "It's going to be a big checkpoint."

"Here?" Robyn said. "Why here? There's nothing here."

Key raised one shoulder. "They must have figured out people are using Sherwood Alley to avoid passing through the checkpoints at Briar and Cross."

"*I* use Sherwood Alley," Robyn grumbled. "How am I supposed to get out of here now?"

"You know how."

She did, and she didn't like it. Key's favorite route out of the old church was what they called "the back way," which involved exiting the church through the alley fire escape and climbing across the Dumpsters that served the storefronts on the next block.

"Anyway, we can't go out now."

"Why not? We need a grocery run."

"We have a rebellion to plan, remember?" Key said. "Everyone will be here soon."

Robyn's stomach swooped a bit at the thought of facing Chazz again.

"Maybe I should just turn myself in," Robyn mused. "If I learned anything last night, it's that the rebellion is already much bigger and stronger without me." She glanced at Key. "You said so yourself."

Key's expression twisted in sorrow. "That's not what I meant."

"We can't save my parents otherwise, can we? We never could." It felt suddenly so obvious and true. That thing she had carried, the relentless bubble of hope inside her, began to fizzle.

"You're always talking about the big picture," she reminded him. "Trade me for them. They can do more to help. It makes sense."

"Never," Key said. "We never surrender."

⊰CHAPTER SIX⊱

Breakfast with Crown

Merryan Crown entered the formal dining room and found her uncle waiting for her.

"Good morning, Merryan, dear."

"Morning." She pulled out her regular chair and scooted in to meet the omelette and fruit that were waiting for her.

It was unusual for her uncle to join her for breakfast. Occasionally they shared a dinner, but those occasions had grown increasingly rare since they'd moved into the governor's mansion. Merryan now had her own suite of rooms. She missed the old house, which was modest by Castle District terms, but still quite large for just the two of them.

He sat across the table now, coolly sipping a mug of coffee. Unsure of how to break the ice, Merryan salted her eggs and began eating.

"How are you this morning?" he asked.

Uncle Iggy had never been especially warm. She knew from the first days after the funeral that he had taken her in out of obligation, or appearances—some sense of propriety that lingered deep within him. Loyalty, maybe. To her father, his brother. Though, given his recent actions around the city, that seemed less likely. Her uncle seemed now to have stripped himself of all kindness and compassion.

Yet here he was, attempting some kind of connection.

"I'm okay," Merryan answered. "Still a little upset over yesterday."

His timing was suspect. Her role in letting Robyn into the mansion had not gone unnoticed. No way he decided separately to talk to her today.

She felt on display. Since he took her in, Merryan had worked hard to become someone who pleased her uncle. Someone whose presence was barely noticeable. She couldn't bear to be sent away. Yet, it was also very hard to be with him, to feel the pressure of living up to his exact standards.

Now, everything was turned upside down. Merryan had risked everything. She drew a deep breath, reminding herself that others, like Robyn, had already lost everything.

"I've not done right by you," her uncle said.

"Oh—" she started to protest.

He stopped her. "Hear me out. You've lost so much, and I haven't always been there."

"Uncle Iggy . . ."

"I'd like us to do more things together."

Maybe he thought he was fooling her. Maybe he thought she couldn't see the truth: that he'd be watching her. Maybe she ignored those things, because a small part of her, deep down underneath, had been hoping someday he would say this.

"I'd like that," she answered, pouring love and hope into her voice. The part of her that wanted to believe . . . But the rest of her knew better. He wanted to keep an eye on her? She wanted to keep an eye on him, too.

Her uncle's face softened just a smidge. Just enough for her to believe the door had finally cracked open. Merryan's usefulness to Robyn and her friends hinged on her access to her uncle. If she could get closer to him, maybe there was hope that he could learn to be kind. Maybe he didn't have to be ruined. Maybe he could be saved.

"What are you thinking, my dear?" her uncle asked softly.

Merryan considered her words carefully. "I'm thinking about kindness," she said finally. "It's not easy to make someone feel better after they've made a big mistake. You're being kind, Uncle Iggy, and that helps me."

His expression was something between a smile and a smirk. "I'm not often accused of kindness, you know."

"People deserve second chances, don't you think?"

"In certain circumstances, I suppose." He mused for a moment. "But certainly not for these supposed friends who have used you so unkindly themselves. The risk of kindness is being taken advantage of, you see."

"Yes, I see."

"Good."

"I could sense that I was helping them in a way I didn't understand, but I thought that was a good thing," Merryan said. "I like helping. I can often see people's pain." She stopped short of adding, *it's hard to look at you sometimes.*

"You have my brother's eyes. My brother's heart." Her uncle reached across the table and cupped her cheek with his cool fingers. The touch was both welcome and unwelcome at once.

"I think Dad would want me to take care of you, too. For us to take care of each other." She meant it, from her heart. She could never erase the care she felt for Uncle Iggy. Or the guilt of working behind his back for the good of them all.

"Pain paves the way to greatness, my dear," he said. "You and I will have everything."

⋖CHAPTER SEVEN⋗

Laurel on the Run

Laurel Dayle raced through the manicured gardens of the governor's mansion.

Exit.

Exit. There had to be one somewhere.

The fence around this part of the property was impossible to scale. The tall wood planks pressed against each other with the tightest of seams. Eight feet up, their tops came to points that stabbed upward.

Laurel pushed on every board, testing for weak spots. *I'm small*, she reminded herself. *You can get out of anywhere when you're small.*

The yard was crawling with guards. Hearing voices again, Laurel ducked toward a set of sculpted bushes. She got down on her hands and knees and scurried into the space between them.

Boots thumped past.

Laurel scrambled out the other side of the bushes. It was no longer so dark. There were only so many places to hide. She moved from bush to bush, away from the fence and toward the mansion. It might be the only way out.

She skirted along the edge of the stone wall, avoiding doorways. She found a long garage door, through which she could see rows of parked motor-pool vehicles.

Where there were cars, there had to be an exit. Laurel slipped through the door and crept along the row of parked limousines. Some appeared to be unlocked. Maybe she could hide in one, and then escape later, when it was off the property. If she was lucky enough not to be spotted in the meantime.

She continued toward the big garage door. One was open to the driveway, spilling in light from the outside.

The garage was not empty. Two men stood near the door that must lead into the mansion.

"We've had a break-in. The standards are no longer acceptable." The gruff, slightly balding man seemed to be in charge.

"Yes, Mr. Shiffley."

"Full motorcade security protocols," Shiffley ordered. "The girl is not to be let out of your sight. Am I clear?"

"Three guards, plus the driver."

"Bulletproof glass."

"That sounds reasonable," Shiffley agreed.

"For the short distance between here and the school, this is more than enough protection. No one will be able to touch her," the guard assured him.

"It is equally important that she not be able to get out," Shiffley said. "Miss Crown has proven to be a . . . weak spot."

"Understood." The security guard pointed to his PalmTab. "Windows and doors controlled from here. For the full motorcade."

Laurel flinched as the car door locked and unlocked beside her ear. The windows scrolled up and down with the touch of the guard's fingers across his palm.

"Very good," Shiffley said. "Carry on."

Whew. Laurel felt lucky for hearing that. A ride out by hiding in the cars would be out of the question. She could too easily be trapped.

The men went back inside.

A few moments later, the door opened again. "Have a good day, Miss Crown," a voice said from within the mansion. Merryan stepped out. Laurel resisted the temptation to run toward her and hug her as hard as she could. She crouched lower behind the car.

"Thank you," Merryan said. She released her backpack from one shoulder and slid into the backseat.

Laurel poked her head up and peered through the glass. Merryan's eyes widened. She reached for the door handle. A reflex. But when she tugged, the door was locked from the inside.

Laurel faced a split-second choice. Wait all day until Merryan came home, and hope to get help from her. Or make a break for it.

Merryan's worried face in the rear window made the decision for her. As the limo rolled out, Laurel ran along behind it. She bent forward, keeping her head below the windows.

The guard in his hut pressed a button and waved to the limo driver. Laurel edged along the car's rear bumper, keeping the limo between her and the guard. The gate opened and both the car and the girl on foot zipped through it.

≪CHAPTER EIGHT≫

The Moon Lore

Robyn climbed the stairs to the cathedral choir loft. She looked away from Tucker's piles of research books as she passed the table where he liked to work. He was close to finishing his dissertation, he had said. Would he ever finish now?

Robyn slowed down. Averting her eyes wasn't right. It hurt to look, but maybe it was important. It wouldn't be right to pretend like everything was okay. Not when Tucker had been taken. Given himself to protect the cause. Like Laurel. Like Mom.

There was going to be sacrifice. There was always going to be, in a fight like this.

Robyn had resisted the idea that anything sacrificed would come from her. Her parents. Her own life. Instead, she'd put others at risk to protect what was hers. What kind of leader did that?

Everyone hated Crown because he was selfish. A better governor would put everyone else ahead of himself. A better hoodlum would, too, she supposed. What she had told Key seemed truer than ever. Something would have to be sacrificed. Either her parents, or Robyn herself. That was Crown's ultimatum, and it was a doozy.

Tucker's moon lore books seemed to stare back at her, accusingly. A dozen books, or more. Some from the library, some from his personal collection. He'd studied every aspect of the moon lore, and could tell long (sometimes boring) stories about what was written of the struggles to come.

The books were all tagged and marked with sticky notes poking out of them. They were surrounded by stacks of notebooks, full of Tucker's writings, and an old coffee cup, all dried out and stained.

Robyn turned away again. She didn't have time to get all choked up. She'd dismissed Tucker's knowledge too often. Now, she'd give anything to be able to ask his opinion of what it all meant. Of what might happen next. What *should* happen next.

Robyn moved away from his work station and went to the door of the moon shrine courtyard. Her hand flitted to her chest, feeling for the pendant. The pendant she no longer had. Sheriff Mallet had taken it.

Robyn sighed. Why was she even here? The place drew her to it, much like the fire, but it was pointless to be there. She was unable to get in without the key. So she sat in front of the door and leaned against it. The painted-black metal felt cool against her back. She shivered.

The task ahead of her seemed impossible. Standing by the fire, she'd felt . . . powerful. In control. Like she could take on the governor and the sheriff and the whole lot of MPs that stood against her.

But why? She was only one girl. One girl, with no pendant.

What if all the power was in the pendant? What if that's why she'd been able to convince everyone that she could lead? Maybe what they saw when they looked at her was not anything about herself, but the reflection of the jewelry she happened to own. Even Sheriff Mallet had known the pendant was important and powerful. Why else would she have been so eager to take it for herself?

Robyn rested her head on her knees. Getting the pendant back was probably impossible. Just like saving her parents. The thing to do now was to be strong. Wasn't it? That's what they would want her to do. Keep fighting.

Right below her, a dozen people would soon gather, ready to fight alongside her. Why did she feel more alone than ever?

She reached for her pendant again, reflexively. She had touched and held it a lot, she realized. With that comfort gone, the world seemed a little bit colder. The fire, that much farther away.

In the absence of hope, she was left with faith. Her father had believed in the moon lore, to the very end. He'd planned for his own disappearance, and left her so many clues. The map. The hologram. The pendant.

She pressed her back against the black door. It, at least, had warmed after contact with her body. She didn't even need to read the curtain anymore. She had it memorized:

OFFSPRING OF DARKNESS, DAUGHTER OF LIGHT

GIFTING THE PEOPLE, BEACON INTHE NIGHT

EMERGE AFTER SHADOWS, HIDING HER FACE

HOPE OFTHE ANCIENTS, DISCOVER HER PLACE

BREATH BLOOD BONE, ALL ELEMENTS UNITE

BLAZE FROM WITHIN, INSPIRE THEIR FIGHT

SUN FINDS HOME, IN ANCIENT RUNE

DEEP INTHE CRADLE, OFTHE CRESCENT MOON

Its message was clear.

Clear, but possibly incomplete? Robyn pulled out the new scrap of moon lore cloth and held it. The pendant had led to this moon shrine. Where else might it have led?

The shrines held the key. Suddenly, Robyn was sure of it. Why else would her parents each take such risks in order to give Robyn both halves of the pendant?

Why would the map have been so important to her father? The more time that passed, the more sure she became. There had to be more to the moon lore secrets. Perhaps every answer she was looking for was contained in those scraps of silver fabric.

The way to beat Crown.

The way to find her parents.

The beating heart of the Crescendo, the new Crescent Rebellion.

Robyn touched the still-empty space over her heart. Mallet might have stolen her necklace, but Robyn would find a way to put the pieces together nonetheless.

≪CHAPTER NINE≫

Bullet Points

The gun looked different than Scarlet remembered. It rested in the center of the tabletop. She didn't especially like being alone with it. The weapon was the strongest possible reminder of everything that was wrong.

There was only a short while before Jeb would have to return to the MP barracks, and currently he was using the time to sit in the bathroom for a hundred years. People always made fun of girls for taking a long time in the bathroom. Really, boys were way worse.

Scarlet reached for the gun. It was more glossy than shiny. Still metal, not plastic, but it had a rather plasticky look about it. Like a toy. But she knew it was no toy.

Last night they'd been face to face with Crown's guards. The terror didn't fade so easily. The guards at the mansion had bigger, longer weapons. Rifles, maybe, or some kind of automatic. Big enough to be strapped to them like purses.

Jeb's was handheld, to be worn in a holster at his hip. Each bullet in the cartridge was no bigger than the top of Scarlet's thumb. But that one tiny piece of flying metal was all it would take to destroy her, or anyone she cared about.

She studied the gun closely. It was definitely not the same gun he used to carry. It was about the same size, but lighter. It had grooves where the palm and fingers should rest, and when she held it in her hand, it glowed red along a low mound on the top.

The bathroom door opened. She could hear the fan going for a second before Jeb closed the door behind him. Not fast enough. She still caught a whiff of what he'd been up to in there. Boys.

Scarlet fought the impulse to turn and point the weapon at him. Just as a joke. But she didn't. It wasn't safe. She hated the impulse, even, but guns did that to people, she figured. Brought out your worst instincts. Made you feel reckless. Invincible.

Instead she pointed it at the Wanted poster taped to the wall. At Robyn's sketched-on face. That's what the weapon was meant for, after all. Hunting Robyn. And her friends, including Scarlet herself.

Jeb plopped himself into the chair next to her. Sighing, he reached out and rubbed Scarlet's shoulder with one hand.

"You're okay? You're sure?"

"We got away. No biggie." She pushed away his worry with a grin. "I'm here now."

He gazed upon her skeptically. She was singing a different tune now, that was for sure. It had been a relief to escape from the group and get back to where Jeb was waiting. She had cried. She had scared him at first by not being able to talk about what had happened. And when she finally had, it only filled him with rage and frustration, from which she could barely extract a simmering comfort.

Now, with him sitting there calmly in his MP uniform, comfort seemed like a very faraway thing.

"You don't have to go back," she said. "Be a fugitive, like the rest of us."

Jeb shifted uncomfortably. "It's useful to have me on the inside." He couldn't, wouldn't be the kind of person to fully rebel. Scarlet knew this. *Not everyone has it in them to give up their life for a cause*, Chazz was fond of saying. *But everyone can play a role.*

"Yeah," she said. "Except now it's all falling apart."

"All the more reason to keep myself legitimate."

"I suppose."

"Chazz will have a plan," Jeb assured her. "He always does."

"Or Robyn will." After months of vaguely wishing Robyn would disappear, Scarlet now found herself hoping the little rich girl wouldn't leave them in the lurch. She'd proven herself resourceful. Inspiring.

Then again, if she couldn't handle the truth, maybe they were better off without her. Scarlet lifted the gun again and twitched it at Robyn's poster.

"Aren't you going to tell me not to play with your service weapon?"

Jeb shrugged. "No need. You can't fire it."

"Oh, yeah?" She tucked her finger over the trigger.

"Go ahead, pull it. Nothing will happen." Jeb looked completely calm and unconcerned. Was he bluffing? Obviously she couldn't actually fire the weapon. Not in here.

She lowered it. "What are you talking about?"

"You really shouldn't play with guns," he said.

Scarlet grinned and rolled her eyes. "There it is. I knew you couldn't get by without saying it."

Jeb shook his head. "Ours have safety measures, but they're special. It's not a good habit to get into."

Scarlet laughed. "You sound like an old man. 'It's not a good habit to get into,'" she mimicked. "Give me a break."

"Scarlet. Come on."

"Relax, I know enough not to shoot you," she said. "I would never even point it at you. That's how accidents happen." She winked at him.

Jeb lifted the gun out of her hand by the barrel. "It's not a joke," he said. "I have to, you know, they're teaching me . . . I might have to actually use it."

"You wouldn't," she said, feeling strangely confident.

Jeb's eyes grew sad. "It's my job."

She didn't like him saying it. Didn't want to believe he could ever become what the MPs wanted to make him. He never wanted this life, but he didn't have a choice. Winning Iron Teen, it turned out, was a one-way ticket into law enforcement.

"I guess they did the contest anyway, huh?" Scarlet said. They'd screwed up the winner's dinner last night, but knowing Nott City, the show would go on.

"They're doing it right now," Jeb said. "I'm supposed to be there when it's over."

He laid the gun on the table. He patted the handle as if trying to befriend the deadly thing. When he touched it, the mound along the top glowed green.

"Hey," she said. "It's different."

Jeb nodded. "Safety measures. It reads my finger and palm print. I meant it before when I said you could pull the trigger and nothing would happen."

"So, only you can fire your gun?"

"Well, any MP. We don't have personalized weapons yet. Not at my level. The higher-ups might. I heard that their gun grips are molded based on their actual hands, too."

Scarlet picked up the gun again. The top ridge glowed red. "That's messed up," she declared, tossing it onto the table.

"It's gun control," he said. "It's how we make sure to keep deadly weapons out of the hands of children. And people who shouldn't have them."

Scarlet leaned close to his ear. "Like members of the rebellion?"

"Exactly." Jeb smiled. "Those hoodlums can't be trusted." He turned his head to face hers, and kissed her.

But instead of kissing him back, she pulled away, a puzzled expression on her face. "Hey, how does it know you're touching it? I mean, how does it know it's you?" The puzzle-solving side of Scarlet's brain kicked in.

"Some kind of chip," Jeb said. "We're all in the database."

"So, it's not just pre-programmed. It's wirelessly tied to the network?"

"I don't know," he said, fidgeting. "I pick it up and it works. I don't ask questions."

Scarlet could tell he was frustrated by *her* questions. Jeb liked concrete things he could see and touch. She was the techie, the one whose life revolved around ones and zeroes and machines and invisible forces. He didn't know, but she could find out.

Scarlet ran her hand over his hair. "Computerized weapons? What will they think of next?" She sighed.

Jeb took her hand. "We're going to make things better," he said.

"The MPs?" she scoffed. "Not likely."

"No, us." He kissed her again. She put her hands over his shoulders.

"You're not allowed to do that while you're in the outfit," she reminded him. "I feel like I'm kissing the enemy."

"I have to go, anyway," he said. "When I'm back, we go to the cathedral?"

"I'm going now," Scarlet said. "To see if there's still a rebellion to return to."

"You should wait for me."

Scarlet made a face. "I don't need a big bad gun to protect me," she insisted. "I do fine on my own."

Jeb sighed and stood up. She watched him latch the gun into his hip holster. As she hugged him good-bye, her mind spun around the idea of computers in guns. All the possibilities.

≪CHAPTER TEN≫

Rumors

The rutted bed of the pickup truck was perfectly clean and white. The sun gleamed off it awkwardly. Tucker Branch rolled and jounced along. His shoulder, hip, and temple throbbed from repeated jouncing. His hands and feet were bound together behind him, like an animal headed to slaughter. At least, that's how he felt. Tucker really had no idea how animals looked while headed to slaughter. Maybe they weren't tied up at all. Maybe they all just walked down the road, and into the slaughter-house, as if they were going on a field trip. Not knowing their fate.

Tucker knew his fate. At least, he knew enough that he wouldn't go willingly.

"Is this really necessary?" he'd said as the MPs bound his ankles and wrists, then forced him to bend his knees so they could tie the two together.

The MPs had muttered sounds, short grunts not quite interchangeable with laughter. "No more tricks, Sherwood boy. You're done."

The truck took a sharp turn. *Done.* Tucker closed his eyes and prayed.

The white truck stopped and the engine rumbled down to silence. Tucker's body continued to vibrate. Sounds of voices and machinery filled the void of the engine noise in his ears. The sounds of scraping, sweeping, and shoveling came from all sides.

They pulled him out of the truck, untied him. The impulse to break free and run was squelched by the sight before him.

The massive quarry was surrounded by a thin barbed-wire fence.

He was a prisoner. The worst-case scenario was now a reality.

"Come on, Sherwood boy," the MP said. "This is where you live now."

$$\ggg\!\longrightarrow$$

Sheriff Marissa Mallet sat quietly in her office, high in the Sherwood MP Headquarters. Her picture window looked out over the city, and to the forest beyond.

She held up the pendant in her hand. The white stone circle glowed in the sunlight. Nestled around it, a crescent-shaped black stone. Mallet had retrieved the item from Robyn's own neck. The spoils of war.

The pendant was small, but heavier than she expected. She let it rest in the palm of her hand, feeling the weight of it.

The one who wields the Pendant of Power.

A child of Shadows and Light.

The hoodlum Robyn might fancy herself a leader, but those were girlish fantasies. A whole city, relying on the whims and wishes of a child? No. Mallet herself was the one with all the power. And now she had the pendant to back it up.

Mallet stroked the stones, alternately cool and warm to the touch. She could feel their power. The pendant itself, she had thought to be a myth. A legend. A holdover from the days when the people let the tenets of an obscure faith guide their paths.

But the pendant existed. What did that mean about the rest of the teachings? Had any of the moon lore texts survived? Mallet's heart beat faster at the thought.

Did the shrines exist? Such myths, such rumors, could not really be trusted, could they?

Mallet smiled.

Rumors of a coup.

Rumors of a teenaged hoodlum.

A great many powerful truths had been preceded by rumors.

≪CHAPTER ELEVEN≫

The Crescendo

The cathedral fell quiet. Everyone waited for Robyn to speak. Everyone included Key, Scarlet, Chazz, Nessa Croft, Floyd Bridger, and two men and six women Robyn didn't recognize.

In the great arching space of the cathedral, the group seemed small, even though more people had arrived than she expected.

"I don't know everyone here," Robyn said.

The adults introduced themselves. One woman spoke, "We are the remaining few who started this Crescendo and have not yet been imprisoned."

The "yet" echoed through the air, seeming to bounce off every pillar and arch.

Another said, "Together we all represent the past, present, and future of the Crescent Rebellion. Watching you these past few months, I feel renewed hope."

"Then why did you lie to me?" Robyn couldn't help the question.

"You can't see what you're not ready for," Chazz said. "You know there was a movement. Why weren't you looking to see what had gone before?"

"I thought all the leaders were imprisoned. I saw Nyna Campbell tied up on that stage. I saw the wanted posters for Nessa and Bridger." Robyn nodded to him. "I saw it all the day we first met. I thought we were alone in seeing what needed to be done."

"You came to see me in T.C."

"And you tried to send me packing," she accused Chazz. "You told me flat out to run, that it was useless to stay and fight."

Chazz gazed back at her, seemingly emotionless.

"Now Crown's threatening my parents. I think he's figured out who I am."

Chazz reacted to that. "Then let's focus on the problem at hand. How do we get them out?"

"What did Crown really say?" Key argued. "He didn't mention your parents specifically. He didn't even say *they*. He said *it*."

Robyn recited the message for those who had not heard it firsthand.

"That's vague. He might have been bluffing," Scarlet agreed.

"He could be trying to trick you into turning yourself in," Key said.

No. Robyn knew she had screwed up. She'd called out *Mom* when the guards had grabbed her mother. It would be very easy to put those pieces together. Even for the most thick-headed MPs. With her parents still in Crown's custody, she couldn't take the chance.

"I don't think he's bluffing," Robyn said. She pulled a long slow breath into her lungs. She knew what came next, but it was the hardest thing she'd ever had to utter.

"My parents would want the rebellion to continue," Robyn said. "With or without them." It was especially hard to choke out the last bit. For months now, her sole goal had been to save them. The knot in her chest refused to go away.

But things were different now.

She had watched her mother sacrifice herself for the cause. Robyn understood now what her purpose was. What it all meant.

Robyn's limbs felt heavy. She stood rooted to the spot on the altar. Finally, she forced the weightiest thoughts into words.

"In seventy-two hours, my parents will be killed. We can't stage a rescue in that short a time. But we can send Crown a message."

"What kind of message?" Scarlet asked.

"The message that we are not scared. That this rebellion cannot be crushed by his threats." Robyn paced along the altar. "He knows who I am. He thinks all I care about is my parents. Well, he can destroy my parents, he can destroy me, but he cannot actually win."

"We just keep doing what we've been doing," Key agreed. "Righting wrongs and making a disruption in the biggest possible ways."

Robyn looked to him in relief. That was a good way of putting it. "Yes. If we show him that the rebellion is bigger than Robyn Hoodlum, he'll realize it is pointless to kill my parents."

"Do you really think that's going to work?" Scarlet said.

"It has to," Robyn whispered. The other remaining possibilities were bleak. "He won't kill them when he sees what we're capable of." She spoke more confidently than she felt.

"Nonsense, girlie," Chazz barked. "The threat is specific. It's different now."

"Yes, it's different," Robyn said.

"By the moon," Chazz thundered. "We need a new plan for breaking them out. This is what you've wanted all these months. Now the rest of us are on board, and suddenly you change your tune? We go back in and save them."

Nessa put a hand on his shoulder. "I think Robert would be the first to agree with Robyn. We need to motivate more people to be involved before we can hope to do anything for the Loxleys."

It was the first time her parents' names had been spoken aloud, even in this small group. Robyn surrendered to another wave of feeling foolish. She'd thought she was so anonymous and mysterious. But Chazz and Nessa, and maybe the others, had known exactly who she was all along.

"We've got thousands of people working in Block Six every day. Now's the time to get serious about that army!" Chazz said.

"We're at our best when we work as a team," Key said.

"That's what Crown needs to see," Robyn agreed. "All of us. Coming right for him."

"Ready to take him down." Key's voice grew deeply insistent.

Robyn stood tall before them. Her job as a leader of the movement was one thing. Her responsibility as a daughter was another. Chazz was right—she'd find a way to save her parents somehow, even if it meant walking straight into Crown's office and taking his deal. But the movement was bigger than all of them. In the meantime, it made sense to keep the Crescendo alive. Her parents would need something to return to, after all was said and done.

"Stop," she said, commanding all the authority she could into her voice.

The room fell quiet. *Huh. It worked*, Robyn thought. She filled her lungs with new air and began.

"We need to send Crown a message. A message of solidarity from all the people of Sherwood. Something to convince him that killing my parents, or any of those imprisoned, would result in massive uprising from the people."

"We have only three days," Scarlet said. "Something like that could take months."

"Are we thinking of a giant protest or demonstration?" said one of the women.

"Not sure," Robyn said, speaking from her gut. "I think we're looking for something smaller and easier to pull off in a short time."

"But something very public," Nessa Croft suggested. "Tomorrow there will be the weekly showcase in Block Six. Hundreds of people will already be gathered. That would be a good time for a mass protest action."

"Showcase?" Robyn asked. "What's that?"

The room was lulled into a respectful but uncomfortable silence.

"Crown's latest intimidation tactic," Chazz grumbled. "It's not enough that people are broke and hungry and struggling, he wants them to be scared to death to boot."

Robyn nodded, even though he had not answered the actual question. Typical of Chazz. And now she was embarrassed to admit she didn't understand. She was supposed to be in charge.

"Can we get enough of the workers on board by then?" Key asked. He turned toward Chazz. "How hard will it be to spread the word?"

"I know the folks who can get it done," Chazz confirmed. "I have several contacts who work construction and sanitation. I know a couple of machinists and a bus driver who's pretty influential among transit workers. We can get the word out, if we know what we want them to do."

"Preferably something that won't result in mass arrests," one of the women said. Murmurs of agreement spread over the room.

"That's a tall order," Scarlet said. "There are always a ton of MPs keeping an eye on the crowd. But if they did something small, we could use it to give hope to all of Sherwood."

"We'll think about it." Nessa shrugged. "I can call for the action in my broadcast tonight."

A picture of this showcase formed in Robyn's mind. Lots of working people, gathered in one place, with MPs monitoring them. She imagined it would be similar to the crowd in which she'd met Bridger. When Mallet had stood on the stage issuing threats, trying to flush out the remaining Crescendo leaders.

"It's not enough," Key said. "And not fast enough. We only have three days. We can't waste all of today and tonight."

Smaller, faster actions. Robyn closed her eyes. "Imagine," she said. "MPs walking through Sherwood, feeling afraid that anyone they pass might be against them. Imagine Crown feeling like everywhere he looks, Sherwood is constantly reminding him that we are ready to fight. What does that look like?"

"A lot of signs?" Key suggested.

"Signs are expensive," Chazz growled.

"A lot of cheap signs?" Key quipped back. "Sticky notes on every window?"

"Too small. Too expensive," Chazz insisted.

"Are people forgetting that we're THIEVES?" Scarlet groaned. "For crying out loud."

"I like that idea, though," Robyn said. "Sticky notes everywhere. In so many places that I couldn't possibly have done it all myself." She paced along the altar. "Between now and the deadline, we do everything we can to show Crown that Robyn is bigger than one girl. She has the support of hundreds, of thousands."

Nessa nodded. "They need to believe we're everywhere."

"We *are* everywhere."

Everyone turned to look at Chazz. He lifted a shoulder, in his laconic way. "We need to believe it, too." He spoke with quiet certainty. A steady confidence that filled Robyn with confidence, too.

"So how can we show that?" Robyn asked. "How can we make the fifteen people in this room seem like hundreds? Because the bigger we look, the bigger we'll actually be." She knew this was true because she'd seen it happen in her old school lots and lots of times. Someone would come in with something new and strange: a hairdo, an accessory, a toy . . . and suddenly, within a few days everyone in class felt they MUST HAVE IT, too. Of course, that had never really worked for Robyn—people just thought she was weird!—but she knew it worked in concept.

"I agree," said Nessa. "People want to do what they think everyone else is already doing. If we look bigger, we become hundreds."

"How about graffiti?" Scarlet suggested. "We tag, all day and all night, in all different neighborhoods. By the time the sun comes up tomorrow, it could look like all of Sherwood rose up to support you."

"Perfect," Robyn said. "We steal a lot of paint, and go to town."

"A lot of GREEN paint, I'd say," Key added.

"I can do it over the night," Bridger said. "But I'm no kind of artist. What will we have to paint?"

"We have no shortage of symbols," Robyn said, growing more and more excited about the idea. "The elements: earth, air, and water. The moon. The fire. The arrow."

"But we want it to be uniform, right?" Key said. "So it's clearly related to you?"

"The arrows," Scarlet said. "Easy to draw, and easy to recognize."

"We paint arrows on everything," Robyn confirmed. "Nessa's broadcast spreads the word, and invites more people to join us in painting."

"And also to protest at the showcase?" Nessa asked.

Robyn didn't totally understand what the showcase actually was; there was time to figure out those details. "I think so," she said. "Let's talk after this meeting."

Nessa nodded in agreement.

"I have an idea about it," Scarlet said. "The three of us can chat."

"Okay," Robyn said. Her first leadership meeting was going pretty well, and she wanted to end it on a high note. They quickly brainstormed places to "shop" for green paint, and divided the responsibility for each neighborhood in Sherwood.

"This afternoon we shop, and tonight, we paint!" Robyn declared. "Tomorrow afternoon, we meet back here."

In response, everyone raised murmurs of agreement and excitement. So Robyn decided the meeting was finished. "For Sherwood, unite!" she said.

Every voice was with her in the refrain. "For Sherwood, we fight!"

≪CHAPTER TWELVE≫

Lost

Laurel walked the wide sidewalks of Castle District slowly. Inside the governor's mansion gates had been scary. Outside the gates was scarier. Every road looked like every other road. The signs had letters and words on them but Laurel couldn't tell what they said. She had no idea which way to walk. She had no idea where there might be checkpoints. There were fewer easy places to hide.

The streets were different here in Castle District. Many of the roads were as wide as the Sherwood Cannonway.

The buildings were different, too. All the houses were separate from each other with big lawns in between. There were no alleys, no fire escapes. There was no way to climb from roof to roof, like she was used to.

She knew she needed to find the woods. There were trees everywhere—in the boulevards, in the parking lots, in people's lawns—but not enough trees together to look like the Notting Wood.

None of the streets seemed like back roads. Laurel kept crossing major streets, fearing MPs, but not seeing any.

Here, it seemed, you could walk freely. Here people left things outside that would be so easy to walk away with. Bikes and radios and hats and baskets and television screens mounted outdoors. Even from the sidewalk she could see lots of interesting things on porches. Hardly any people were walking on the sidewalks, either, but there were lots and lots of cars.

No one seemed to notice her. No one seemed to be looking. It was an entirely different world.

>>⟶

Tucker was sent to join a group of men working in the quarry. A dozen or so guys, equipped with shovels and diggers, wheelbarrows and pickaxes. None of the men looked like they'd been doing this kind of hard labor all their lives. They moved slowly, lifting small shovelfuls of gravel at a time.

Tucker moved toward one of the closest men, who was rolling a wheelbarrow. He joined him, taking one handle to share the load.

"I'm Tucker."

"Robert," the other man said.

Together they eased the wheelbarrow along the bumpy ground. Robert, it turned out, was one of the people taken on the Night of Shadows, as the people of Sherwood called it. The night Crown had staged his coup and taken over. Robert was a former member of Parliament, now ousted from his post.

"Why do they keep the men and women separately?" Tucker asked. It was something he'd been wondering for a while, actually. The previous evening they'd broken into the dungeon in the governor's mansion, to find only the women prisoners. Here, at the gravel camp, it seemed to be all men.

"It's not clear," Robert said. "My theory?" He glanced over his shoulder to make sure they weren't overheard. "Deep down, Ignomus is a softie when it comes to women. Wants to protect them."

Tucker couldn't stop the chuckle that burst forth. "Oh, right. That sounds like him."

Crown? A soft spot for women? Was this the same guy who spends his time hunting and threatening a twelve-year-old girl?

"You've been in prison for months. Do you know what's going on out there?"

Robert also grinned. "That far-fetched, huh?"

"Crown's got a vendetta against a kid. A girl."

"Then he's truly not the man he once was," Robert said, his voice tinged with a great sadness.

Tucker shook his head. Images of Crown's video broadcasts flashed through his mind. "I can't imagine he was ever different."

"He lost his wife some time ago," Robert said. He stabbed the rocks with the shovel blade, then stacked his hands on the rounded tip of the handle. "It—well, it destroyed him." The man's expression turned wistful, gazing off into space. "We were friends back then."

Moments passed. Tucker didn't know what to say. Something spiritual. Something . . . hopeful. He searched his mind, but not fast enough.

Finally, Robert shrugged and began shoveling in earnest. "I can't explain who he's become. And I've spent the last few years trying to prevent him from becoming . . . this."

"Have faith," Tucker said. "We're working on it."

"It's going to take more than a couple of kids to take him down."

"Robyn's tough. She's gonna make it."

Robert's hands slipped off the shovel. The rocks cascaded back into place as the tool clattered to the ground. His dark eyes flashed. "Robyn?"

≪CHAPTER THIRTEEN≫

Intentions

Not long after the Crescendo meeting ended, Robyn sat alone in the cathedral. Nessa and Scarlet had gone their separate ways. The high of leadership was fading, and Robyn found herself feeling small and hopeless once again.

For a moment, surrounded by friends and seeing the faces of those who had come to provide help, she had felt powerful. As powerful as the fire, perhaps.

But in the sudden large quiet, all her doubts crept back in. Would it really be enough?

She would go now, and get some green paint. That would be easy enough. They'd all gotten good at sneaking in and out of Crown's food depots. The new hardware depots that carried things like paint were far less protected at this point. Of course, they would avoid stealing from local businesses if they could help it. The adults would use whatever money they had to buy paint from those business owners. *We steal from Crown, not from the people*, Robyn had reminded them all as they left.

She looked toward the choir loft. Not now. Not yet. The Crescendo had to take priority. First she'd get the paint, then she could study the moon lore. Then she could work on a real plan to save them.

>>>→

Merryan jumped out of the car as soon as it crossed the threshold of the garage and came to a complete stop. She had to tug the car door handle three times before it released. Strange. It hadn't opened that morning to let Laurel into the car, either. She would forever regret not being able to help her friend out of a jam.

Merryan stood outside the car for one long moment, waiting to see if Laurel emerged again. She had seen her running toward the exit, but the car had so quickly left her in its dust, Merryan had no idea if Laurel's escape had worked. She closed her eyes and prayed for the hundredth time today that Laurel was safe.

"I'll be right back," she told her driver as she scooted toward the house. She would run inside, change clothes, and be ready to go again. Today was her after-school volunteer shift at the Sherwood Health Clinic. Of course, she planned to make a secret detour to Nottingham Cathedral during her time in Sherwood. She had to know everyone was okay.

She ran up to her room in record time, dumped her backpack, and stripped off her school uniform. Within minutes she was dressed in the cute outfit she had planned out the night before: a pale green shirt, light-weight skirt, and tights with boots.

But when she returned to the garage, she found the door locked. She stood in the foyer for a moment, con-fused. Her driver appeared, coming through the service entrance—the space where the drivers and security staff had their lockers and their break room.

"Uh, Miss Crown," he said nervously. "The governor would like to see you in his office."

"Can I talk to him later? We're going to be late," she responded.

The driver shrugged, looking even more uncomfort-able. "He said, now."

Merryan resisted the temptation to argue further. He was only doing his job. With a heavy heart, she tromped up the stairs and wound through the hall-ways to reach her uncle's office.

She entered without knocking, which may have been a mistake. Uncle Iggy looked up in surprise as she came through the door. "You wanted to see me?"

Her uncle leaned back in his chair. "How was your day?" he asked.

"So far so good," Merryan said as cheerfully as pos-sible. "But it's only half over. I'm on my way back out."

He frowned. "Merryan, dear, there's been a bit of unrest in Sherwood of late. I'm afraid I'm not entirely comfortable sending you down there."

"But, I'm expected for my volunteer shift," she said. "They're counting on me." She hoped her voice did not give away the undercurrent of anxiety and panic coursing through her. What if she couldn't get back to see Robyn, to make sure everyone got away all right? She was dying to ask her uncle what all had happened, but of course she could not.

Crown nodded. "I've called the clinic to let them know you can't make it today."

"What?" How could he do that without telling her?

"It's not a good idea right now for you to be leaving the Castle District."

"Why on earth not?" she asked, her voice rising in annoyance. She tried to tamp it down. Tried to remind herself that she wasn't supposed to know any of what was going on. She was an innocent bystander.

"There are many people . . ." He paused. "Your safety is paramount, my dear."

"I'm safe. It's perfectly safe," Merryan insisted. "I volunteer at the health clinic."

"At one point you were doing some tutoring, closer to home. What happened with that?"

"That's later in the week," she told him. She tutored a couple of kids from her school in math and history.

She was surprised her uncle knew anything about her volunteer work, or cared.

"Tutoring seems like a good use of your skills. Perhaps you could do more of that? You're a very smart girl, Merryan."

"Yes, thank you." Merryan racked her brain for other things to say. What else could she try? She put on a distressed expression. "Uncle Iggy, is this—is this because—because of the mistake I made?"

His expression stayed motionless, perfect. It was impossible to read his thoughts. "Merryan, dear, everyone makes mistakes." He paused. "But it's true, I don't like the way that these children took advantage of you. I don't want you at risk."

"But—" She had to get back to Sherwood. "You could come with me. You'd see that there's nothing to be afraid of."

Her uncle studied her thoughtfully.

"You said you wanted to be closer to me," she said, grasping for straws. "Maybe it would be good for you to see what I do with my time."

"You know what I haven't done in a long while?" her uncle said suddenly. "Go to the movies!"

The change of subject caught Merryan off guard. "What?"

"Let's find out what's playing," he suggested cheerfully.

"Why don't you want me to go to Sherwood?"

"We can make an afternoon of it. Popcorn? The works!" He was reaching for the intercom button. He seemed overly excited.

Merryan was at a loss for what to do.

Did Uncle Iggy think she could be distracted so easily from the things she cared about? He was playing with her heart surely enough. The truth was, she had always wanted them to do things together. The part of her that wanted to fight was rivaled by the part of her that wanted to play along and pretend things were okay.

"Um, okay," she said.

$$\ggg\!\!\longrightarrow$$

Sheriff Mallet's control console was smooth white and silver, covered in touch screens. The desk's flat surface angled up forty-five degrees to face her as she rested in her high-backed white leather chair.

Occasionally, as now, she ran a manicured finger along the edge of the desk, simply celebrating its power. From here, she could access whatever information she needed about any registered business, organization, or individual in all of Sherwood, and much of the rest of Nott City.

A city-wide search had brought up very little in relation to the moon lore. A couple of fringe websites. A couple of herbal products meant to help you sleep. And a fairly significant collection of classic books in the Sherwood Public Library.

Mallet clicked through the other websites quickly, offering them only perfunctory attention. Then she entered the library database. Libraries were useful places.

The database returned a listing of several books relating to the moon lore. Mallet zipped the list of call numbers over to her PalmTab, then pushed back from the desk. It would be harder to explain to an aide why she wanted what she wanted. Better to go down there herself.

⊰CHAPTER FOURTEEN⊱

Best-Laid Plans

When the circuit board sensors were tripped, a beeping alarm went off inside the cathedral. Robyn left her fresh stash of green paint in the office with Key. She scurried to the edge of the stairs and looked down at the secret entrance.

Jeb strolled in, wearing his MP uniform. Scarlet was right behind him. Darn. Their entrance meant her own departure must be delayed slightly. She had made a plan to meet up with Bridger soon, but in the meantime she had meant to explore the moon lore clues on her own. She wouldn't start tagging until after dark, but she planned to use the rest of the afternoon wisely.

"Don't you work today?" Robyn asked as Jeb got closer.

"It's my lunch break."

"Jeb told me something interesting today," Scarlet reported.

"Oh, yeah?" Robyn waited on the landing as they climbed the stairs to meet her. They were also carrying paint, concealed in canvas sacks. She relieved them of some of the load.

"All of the MPs' weapons are being systematically replaced," Scarlet continued.

"Bigger, badder, more deadly?" Robyn quipped.

"Pretty much," Jeb confirmed. "The new sidearms are completely awesome."

"Try to say that with a little less enthusiasm, eh?" Scarlet said. Together they moved down the hall.

"What's happening to the old ones?" Key said as the others entered the office. He sat behind the piles of green paint canisters on the desk, staring at a sketchy map of Block Six that Bridger had drawn.

"Funny you should ask," Jeb said. "I just looked into it."

"They're being dumped in a warehouse here in Sherwood." Scarlet spread her arms wide. "A giant container."

Jeb nodded. "In a couple of days, once the change-over is complete, they'll all be taken to the foundry and melted down."

"Not if we get to them first," Scarlet said, her brows folding in determination.

"Get to them how?" Key asked.

"Break in and steal them!" Scarlet hitched her thumb toward him. "Where has he been all our lives?"

Robyn grinned. Key looked sheepish. "Yeah, yeah."

"It's not a good idea," Jeb said.

Scarlet crossed her arms. "Sure it is."

"What are we going to do with all those guns?" Robyn asked. "What's the point of taking them?"

"It's new," said Scarlet. "It takes our rebellion up a notch. And shows we're serious."

"This isn't the kind of rebellion we are," Jeb said. "There are other ways to take down Crown."

"Then why did you even bring it up?" Scarlet retorted.

Jeb crossed his arms. "I didn't. I mean, not for this. I was just . . . telling you about my day."

"We're not looking to fight a war in the streets," Robyn said. "We can't win that way."

"It may come to that," Key argued. "Down the road."

"Us versus the MPs?" Robyn was skeptical.

"We'd have to take time to train," Jeb argued. "We have some experienced people in our ranks, but still. That takes a lot of time and organizing."

"Crown's not going to roll over because of childish tricks," Key said. "Does anyone really think he's going to?"

Scarlet nodded. "We stole some food. Big whoop. So far we're helping people get by day to day, but the Crescendo should be about making real change."

Key slammed a fist into his palm. "Ousting Crown."

"That's a long way away," Robyn said quietly. "That's what the prison breaks were about. Freeing the people who could actually lead us."

"Well, we failed," Key said. "We couldn't save them all. And that leaves us in charge."

The other three looked at Robyn.

This was the kind of moment when a leader was supposed to stand up.

She was already standing. What was she supposed to do next?

Her plan for today had been pretty straightforward—try to find out as much as she could about the missing pieces of the moon lore. Meeting with Bridger was only the first step. She had to study Tucker's books, and try to locate the other shrines. And then tonight, paint the arrows.

But Key, Scarlet, and Jeb were staring expectantly at her. Robyn's mind worked the problem.

Hundreds, maybe thousands of guns. Waiting to be melted.

Weapons.

A way to show the MPs they wouldn't always have the upper hand. That seemed important. Robyn had to think about what was best for the Crescendo. She had promised them she would no longer put herself first. Missing guns plus walls full of arrows? That was bound to unsettle the powers that be.

"It doesn't matter if we never plan to use the guns," Robyn said slowly. "It'll frighten the MPs just to know that we have them."

Key, Jeb, and Scarlet exchanged glances. "Sure," Key said.

"It would," Jeb agreed reluctantly.

"We don't have to use them," Scarlet said. "But think of the message it sends. The power it promises."

She was right about that. Crown was so fixated on hunting Robyn that perhaps he'd forgotten the truth: the rebellion was much bigger than one girl. Maybe a score like this would be enough to take some focus off her and her parents.

"Okay," said Robyn. "This fits our goal. We need to remind Crown that we are more than what he thinks we are. He wants to take me down, but this is only the beginning. We want him to imagine all the people who might be receiving those guns, and what they might do with them."

"We are many," Jeb agreed. "Sorry, I have to get back to work." He handed them a folded piece of paper, pencil-sketched. A map of the warehouse location.

Robyn narrowed her eyes at him. "You came with a map already drawn? You knew we would decide to do this."

Jeb turned his palms to the ceiling and coughed a little chuckle. Then he kissed Scarlet's cheek, waved, and ducked out.

"How will we get the guns out?" Scarlet asked. "Another truck?"

Robyn grinned. "We've gotten good at boosting trucks."

"But you haven't gotten any better at driving them," Key pointed out.

"Hey." Robyn pouted. "We all survived, didn't we?"

"Not all," Key said quietly.

Robyn flushed with shame. "You know what I meant." Of course she couldn't forget how they'd lost Laurel and Tucker. How she had jumped behind the wheel and cemented the decision to leave them to the MPs. She suffered for it.

Key chucked her on the shoulder. "Don't feel bad. We are all willing to sacrifice ourselves for the rebellion."

Try not to forget you said that, Robyn thought. She shook her head. "I don't want to sacrifice anyone."

Key didn't respond and Robyn was grateful. They left the truth unspoken: sacrifice had always been needed to make changes happen. Sacrifices would surely be needed again.

"Is it too big a risk to try trucks again?" Robyn mused.

"With all the new checkpoints, it's going to be hard to find a clean path away from the factory," Key agreed.

"Not to mention a safe place to dump them where we can walk away."

They studied the map Jeb had given them. "Look at how close to Block Six it is," Scarlet said. "There are probably a half dozen checkpoints in the vicinity."

"We can only get lucky so many times," Robyn reminded them. "This time, it'd be better to go in on foot."

"Hundreds of guns? That's a lot of weight to carry."

"We're not a small group alone anymore," Scarlet reminded her. "We can call on all of Sherwood."

"Nessa's ready to broadcast," Key said. "She can get us volunteers. We just have to decide where and when we need them."

"Nessa's working on the showcase protest," Scarlet said. "We should take care of this ourselves. Today."

Robyn sighed. Her vision of spending the afternoon hunting moon shrines burst like a bubble of soap. Scarlet was right. Now was the time. "They might move the guns again," Robyn said. "Anyway it's a pretty strong statement if we pull a big heist the same day Crown delivers an ultimatum against me."

"True," Key agreed. "But we need more bodies if we're going to pull this off."

"I have an idea," Robyn said. "No broadcast needed."

≪CHAPTER FIFTEEN≫

A Store So Big

Laurel stood in the parking lot of the biggest store she had ever seen. The store was so large it took up a whole city block. The block was so long, it would have been two or three blocks, in Sherwood.

She wanted to go inside. Stores were usually safe enough, right?

Laurel didn't have any money. She was very good at sneakily borrowing things from small simple stores, but she could tell from the store's big fancy entryway that it would be very hard for her to shop here.

Still. Laurel loved shopping. It was too hard to pass up the chance to see what such a big store looked like on the inside. She darted through the sliding glass doors, straight into retail heaven.

The superstore had forty aisles. Laurel strolled through all of them, one by one. They seemed to sell everything here. It was a grocery store, and a clothes store, and an auto shop, and a drug store, and a toy store all in one.

Laurel gazed longingly at a blue and black bicycle with red and orange flames on the bars. She stood next to it and squeezed the rubber handles. Something like this would get her back to Sherwood much faster.

"Where is your mother?" said a man in a bright red vest. He loomed over her like a tree that had suddenly sprouted from the tile. "If it's okay with her, you can take it for a test ride."

Laurel scampered away quickly. She didn't know how to ride a bike. Unless you counted clinging to the back of Robyn when they rode the moped Robyn's dad had left for her.

Laurel turned in to an aisle full of camping gear. There were some hammocks and a couple tents of different sizes, all set up for people to try. All of these things would be very useful back in T.C.

Laurel sighed. This amazing place would be much more fun to explore if Robyn was here.

She returned to the food section. She had an idea. It would be impossible to take anything out through the scanning exit doors, but she could take it someplace else. The store was so big that many of its aisles were empty of people. She strolled through the food section and selected an apple, two bags of flavored chips, and a wrapped turkey sandwich from the deli section. There was a giant cooler of soft drinks, with more varieties than she could recognize. The lettering on the bottles was too hard to read, so she went by the prettiest colors. She picked a lavender-colored drink and one that was bright yellow.

With that, her arms were full. She scurried to the far back of the store near the car parts section. No one was around. The shelves were big and high and full of heavy things like rotors and cans of car wax.

Laurel climbed. All the way to the top of a set of shelves containing windshield wiper blades and tree-shaped air fresheners. They smelled faintly of pine, even through the plastic. It reminded her of home.

She pushed aside extra boxes of the air fresheners to make a small space for herself up high. From here, she could see much of the store. People's heads bobbed through the aisles, and for a moment Laurel felt very conspicuous. But no one really looked up that high while they shopped.

She ate the food she had collected, savoring every bite of the first full meal she'd had in a while. She polished it all off, and stuffed the trash into the empty chip bags.

She was really quite tired at that point. So she curled up, right there on the shelf, and fell asleep.

≪CHAPTER SIXTEEN≻

Impromptu Heist

The swings at the elementary school were low to the ground. Robyn's knees poked up against her chest, as she swayed and twisted, gripping the plastic-coated chains. It was sort of annoying, but it also made her feel large and important. She dug her toes into the gravel and waited.

Beside her Scarlet pushed off, attempting to swing properly. Her heels crashed into the ground immediately. Too low to pump. The girls giggled.

They stood up instead, and leaned against the sloping bars that held the swings off the ground. Scarlet, in her leather jacket, with the dyed-red tips of her black hair poking up over the collar, looked incredibly cool. Robyn hoped her own beret—the one with the braid sewn into it—made her look half as cool.

"We're exactly the sort of ruffians no one wants around a playground," Robyn said.

Scarlet laughed and shrugged. "We're kids. It's cool. It's not like we're peddling drugs or anything."

"Ha. I'm sure they'd say we're peddling something worse."

The after-school bell rang. The muffled metallic sound echoed through the walls and windows.

"Here we go," Scarlet said. She slid off the swing.

Soon, the doors pushed open and children began streaming out into the yard. Some ran straight for the playground equipment, while others fanned out alone or in small groups to walk home.

"Hey," Robyn whispered as the first wave of kids reached the edge of the yard. "Want to help out Robyn Hoodlum?"

Across the schoolyard, Scarlet did the same.

"*Pssst.* Want to help Robyn Hoodlum?"

"Follow us. Keep it quiet, but pass it along."

An excited ripple of murmurs shimmered over the crowd as word passed from child to child. Some, wide-eyed and terrified, scurried in other directions. But most followed along. From their backpacks, Scarlet and Robyn pulled packages of crisped rice treats and handed them out to the kids who joined the procession. They scarfed down the snacks greedily and smiled.

"What do we have to do?" someone asked.

"It'll be easy." Robyn told them. "You ever play bucket brigade?"

"Play what?"

"You'll see," she promised. "It'll be easy, but we need lots of people to help."

They led the children to the area near the factory, and lined them up over the course of several blocks.

"We're going to pass the trash bags down the line, one at a time," Robyn explained the plan over and over to small groups. "Until everyone has a bag. Once you have a bag, then you're going to follow in a line. Okay?"

They nodded.

The code word is "Skedaddle," Robyn told them. "If you hear us scream it, yell it as loud as you can, to pass it down the line. And then run."

"Run where?" one little boy asked. "Anywhere," Robyn said.

"Toward home," Scarlet added. The children nodded again. They were used to following directions, Robyn supposed. And used to standing in a line. It was all going more smoothly than she had expected.

$$\ggg\!\!\longrightarrow$$

The factory spewed foul metal smoke from chimneys.

"Maybe we're too late," Robyn mused.

"I don't think so," Scarlet said. "The whole place is for melting down metal. It's probably someone else's stuff they're destroying."

"Of course."

They lined up the last group of children right outside the factory. They climbed on top of the pile of crates they had prepared, and broke in through a high, cracked window. The inside of the factory was steaming hot. Robyn choked on the molten air. Sweat instantly beaded on her skin.

"Let's not be in here long," Scarlet whispered.

"Let's find the gun bin." Robyn pulled her backpack off her shoulder, and extracted a roll of black garbage bags. Ready to go.

>>>⟶

The thing took time, but went smoothly. It hadn't occurred to the MPs, perhaps, that anyone would want to steal scrap metal. The facility was completely unguarded. There were plenty of workers inside, who Robyn dodged on each run from the container. But they weren't really looking.

Scarlet hauled herself into the container with the guns. She methodically checked that each one had no bullets, the way Jeb had taught her. They had all agreed—the guns must be 100 percent safe if children were carrying them.

She carefully filled the bags, but not too full—each had to fit out the high, narrow window, and be light enough to be carried by a child. The first child in line camped out under the window, and as Robyn scurried over with each pair of bags, the little girl grabbed them and hauled them out the window.

The children outside climbed the crates eagerly, passing the bags down the long line.

At the other end of the line, Key was waiting. When the first bag reached him, he started the procession away from the factory. As they received their bags, one by one, the children scurried along behind him, suddenly and powerfully a part of the rebellion.

≪CHAPTER SEVENTEEN≫

Successful Shopping

Laurel woke with her mouth feeling clammy. She climbed down and made a beeline for the oral hygiene aisle. Even in a store as big as this, it was easy to find a toothbrush and toothpaste. Laurel stood for a long time just staring at the overwhelming selection of products. She had never seen so many fancy toothbrushes. Not to mention the dozen different kinds of dental floss.

There was even a bathroom in this store, but it was very near the customer service counter. Better to wait, Laurel thought, and get outside.

A mother pushed a shopping cart with a three- or four-year-old boy in the child seat at the top. His legs kicked through the holes and his arms flailed everywhere.

While his mom shopped from the list in her hand, the child leaned out of the cart and grabbed things, too.

He swept a whole row of packaged cookies into the basket.

"Not so many, Davey," his mother said absently. But she didn't reach over and put any of it back.

Laurel followed the woman through several aisles. When she wasn't looking, the boy added applesauce, chocolate drops, a package of swirly, fun-looking straws. His mother didn't notice. Surely she would notice at checkout, Laurel figured. But the woman herself was adding lots of items to the cart. Soon, the boy's additions were completely buried. He looked at Laurel and grinned.

Curious, Laurel followed them all the way to the checkout. But of course, there was no checkout. The stores in Castle District, like the newest ones in Sherwood, too, had automatic checkout. Castle District shoppers all had Tags on their hands. They would push the cart in between the doors, and get charged for everything in the space with them. Quick and easy.

Laurel had an idea. When the mom wasn't looking, she stuffed her new backpack onto the shelf over the cart wheels. She stood back and held her breath. The mom pushed the cart through the checkout doors. The outer door opened and she kept walking.

Once the outer doors closed, the inner doors opened again. Laurel entered the checkout chamber. The doors closed around her and she was scanned. Since no items for purchase turned up on her, the outer door opened and Laurel ran through.

She rushed after the harried mom, and caught up to her near a white station wagon. While the woman lifted the squirming little boy out of the cart and buckled him into his car seat, Laurel retrieved her stowaway backpack and ran off through the parking lot.

$$\ggg\!\!\longrightarrow$$

The storeroom behind the braid shop was dusty and full of boxes. They had pretty logos on them, but hadn't been disturbed in a while. Inside the salon, there were only a few customers. People in Sherwood had less and less time for things like haircuts and styling gel.

"Come on," Key said. He nudged the children one by one down the shadow corridor between the shops. They deposited the bags in a pile in the middle of the room. The bulky bags clattered and listed and slouched against each other. A giant, unruly mound.

A giant, unruly mound of death, Key amended his thoughts.

To defeat Crown, it was going to take everything. Key's body flooded with rage and hate and other feelings he refused to name.

The children kept coming. The bags piled up.

One little girl juggled a bag that had somehow sliced open. When she set it against the others, it tore, and the weapons skittered out onto the floor.

"Sorry," she whispered. Then her eyes grew wide at the sight. It occurred to Key then that none of the children probably realized what they had been carrying. The girl stared at him, her mouth rounding.

"Don't tell the others," Key said. "Some people won't understand."

The girl looked uncertain.

"We're here to protect you," Key reminded her. "You did a good thing today."

"For Sherwood, we fight," she said.

"Yes."

She scurried away, leaving Key alone with the spilled guns.

There they lay, cold and vicious even in their stillness.

Key bent and swept them back inside the torn plastic, lest any of the other kids notice them.

The children kept coming. The bags piled up.

Key moved the ripped bag and its contents to the back side of the pile. There was almost enough plastic to tie it in a knot and seal the hole.

He pulled out one gun. There. Easy to tie.

The extra gun lay on the floor, expectantly. He could tuck it away, too, just hide it in the pile. But to defeat Crown, it was going to take everything.

So he slipped it under his shirt, into his waistband.

⟨CHAPTER EIGHTEEN⟩

Arrows in Everything

It wasn't long before the staff inside the braid shop noticed the strange parade. The shop's glass door tinkled open and someone emerged. A young woman with a swirled tiara of hair twined atop her head.

"Can I help you?" she said.

"You're already helping," Key answered.

"Who are you?"

"Eveline knows," he said. "She told us we could use this room if we needed to. How do you think we knew it was here?"

The hairdresser nodded. "I'll tell her you've come."

"It's not me she'll want to talk to," Key said. "It's . . . my friend." He resisted the impulse to use Robyn's name. "She'll be here later."

"Very well," the hairdresser said. Key couldn't help but notice that her forehead furrowed in worry as she spoke.

≫→

There were more gun bags than kids, as it turned out. "The math was never going to be perfect," Scarlet grunted as they shoved the last bags out the factory window themselves.

"What do we do with the excess?" Robyn wondered aloud.

"We can't leave any behind," Scarlet said. "They have to think we cleaned them out totally."

Down the block, there was a regular industrial Dumpster. The girls glanced at each other and shrugged. "Well, they are in trash bags," Robyn said. "Maybe no one will notice."

They hauled the extra sacks a few at a time and heaved them over the side of the metal bin.

"We could've just thrown them all away," Robyn said with regret. "That would've been much easier."

"What if we need them later?" Scarlet said. "It's good to keep our options open."

A chill went down Robyn's spine. She didn't especially want to keep that particular option open. Was that really where they were headed with this rebellion? Toward a battle? An all-out war? It was not going to be easy to take down someone as clever and cruel and powerful as Crown, but Robyn couldn't help but think her parents would want it to happen on their own terms. Peacefully, if possible.

Still, she didn't protest it out loud. Robyn and Scarlet hustled toward the braid shop, carrying the last couple of bags.

Scarlet led the way, cutting through the streets with surprising turns. Every few blocks she stopped at a corner, and peered around a building before they proceeded.

"You've memorized all the checkpoints?" Robyn said. Usually, she took to the rooftops, leaping from building to building and only coming down when she had to cross a wider street.

"No, they keep moving them," Scarlet reminded her. "I'm just looking as we go."

"How are you seeing all that in advance?"

"Look," Scarlet paused at a particular intersection and pointed down the angle of the street. Following her arm, Robyn could see two blocks over and two blocks down, between the buildings. If they continued on this path, and turned right at the next intersection, they'd run into a checkpoint in two blocks. "Everything in Sherwood is built on crazy angles," Scarlet said. "You haven't noticed?"

"I guess not," Robyn admitted. It seemed embarrassingly obvious now that Scarlet had pointed it out. *Study the angles. There are arrows in everything.* Floyd Bridger's words floated back to her.

Robyn stopped suddenly. Maybe he'd meant literal angles. Not metaphorical ones.

"Hang on."

The girls ducked into a recessed doorway. Robyn pulled out the map her dad had left her. *Study the angles.*

There had to be something here.

"Here, look at this," Robyn pointed to Scarlet. "Look at what's marked."

"That's the cathedral," Scarlet said.

"And the fire in Tent City."

Scarlet pointed. "The tree house?"

"Yeah."

The tree house, with its stone base. A possible second shrine? A little bloom of hope opened up inside her.

She had to get back to the tree house to check it out. What if the answer to everything was there?

But first, the braid shop. Robyn grinned. Of course. It had been right under her nose all along.

"What's this?" Scarlet pointed to the twisty icon on the map.

"We're in luck," Robyn said. She folded the fragile paper and tucked it away. "We're already headed that way."

》》⟶

"The library database lists these books," Mallet reported to the woman behind the checkout counter. "I can't find them on the shelves."

The librarian punched some key. "They are checked out," she reported.

"All of them?"

"Yes. I'm sorry."

"When are they due back?"

"Well . . ." The librarian consulted the screen. "Unfortunately, not for several months."

Mallet frowned. "That doesn't sound right. I thought the borrowing period was a couple of weeks?"

"Yes. But they've been checked out by a graduate student working on a thesis. He received special permission to keep these six books longer than normal. I'm very sorry."

"There were seven books. Where is the seventh?"

"It appears to be missing."

"Missing?" Mallet's agitation increased.

The librarian clicked a few more keys. "Yes, and it may have been stolen," she reported. "I'm attempting to track its location based on its barcode, but it doesn't appear to be anywhere in the library."

"Hang on." The librarian disappeared into the office behind the desk. Mallet tapped her fingers on the countertop. This was unacceptable.

The librarian returned moments later with a thick textbook in her hand. "You might try taking a look at this, in the meantime."

Mallet proffered her library card. "Fine. I'll take this one."

The librarian tapped the book's spine. "I'm sorry, Sheriff. I'm afraid that's a reference copy."

"I would like to use it for reference." Mallet smiled engagingly.

The librarian shook her head. "It doesn't circulate. You'll have to use it here in the library." She smiled. "The good news is, you can come back any time to access it, and know that no one else can check it out, either." Her bright, encouraging tone of voice grated on Mallet's mood.

"Very well." She snatched the book off the counter and took it to a nearby table.

The reference book contained only brief mention of moon lore texts. Nothing Mallet didn't already know. She tamped down her frustration and began tapping the screen in her palm.

Her PalmTab had reasonable access to the central databases, but it didn't have everything. The library's records were sealed, she remembered. They had refused to connect their internal system to the city central database, even though it was a mandatory upgrade for all agencies. The library was still on a closed loop. Something to do with privacy for patrons. It had been a big to-do some while ago, but these things fell on some-one else's desk.

It didn't matter. It would be easy enough to find out who checked out the books. Mallet tapped the screen and sent a message to her boys in the basement. Her lab techs could surely open a path to the information she needed.

⟨CHAPTER NINETEEN⟩

Family Reunion

Eveline glided among the salon chairs toward the door.

"What have you done to your beautiful hair?" The older woman's silver braid glittered. Robyn felt a longing for the piece of herself that was missing. Her hand went involuntarily to her bare neck. The fringe of ruffled curls that met her skin still felt unfamiliar.

"I have to talk to you," Robyn blurted out. No time for pleasantries, for sentiment.

Eveline regarded her calmly. "Young people. Always in a rush."

Robyn pushed down her frustration and tried not to be rude. She didn't have time to mess around. Not when her parents had mere hours left to live.

"It's about the moon lore, and the shrines," she said.

"*Shh.*" Eveline placed her arm around the girl. "Come upstairs with me."

In the small, single-room apartment, Robyn pulled out the map and showed her. "The cathedral, the tree house, this braid shop. That's not a coincidence, is it?"

"The shrines no longer exist. They were destroyed."

"But they still matter," Robyn insisted. "Their messages were supposed to help people figure out what to do."

"That's not quite—"

"I'm figuring it out." Robyn cut her off.

Eveline sighed.

"They built a tree house over the site of the second one." Robyn traced the triangle for her. "According to the map, the third one should be here."

"It is not here," Eveline assured her. The old woman closed her eyes. She hummed softly, a tune Robyn felt in her bones. "But I believe you when you say it once was here. I've long been drawn to this place. And the view of the sky. The full moon passes right over my window."

Robyn looked up at the extra-large pane of glass.

"He's going to kill my parents," she said.

Eveline looked pained. "Yes, I heard the broadcast." Her fingers pressed against each other as if holding on to something that wasn't there.

"My father told me that the braid you wear, the braid I used to wear, is something handed down through my family."

Eveline smiled. "Yes."

"Are you . . . are we related?"

"We are all related, love."

"But I—you—I can see it in your face. Are you . . . my grandmother?"

"No, love," Eveline said. "She was my sister. The youngest of us. The bravest."

So it was true.

"Does my dad know?"

"Your father knows a great many things."

The wise-woman non-answer answer thing was starting to get on Robyn's nerves. Perhaps it showed in her face, because Eveline smiled.

"He knows some about the history of our family."

"Why have I never met you? Why didn't he bring me to Sherwood? I could have known about this all before." Robyn felt ashamed. She'd had a charmed life, free from fear, where she hungered for danger and adventure. Meanwhile, people in Sherwood, people like Laurel, lived skittish and rootless, getting by moment to moment. It didn't seem fair.

Eveline wrapped her arms around Robyn. Her angular figure had enough softness to settle in to.

"Your father is a dear man, with a good heart," she said. "He has not forgotten where he came from. But there are many reasons why it is hard for him to return."

"He always says family is everything."

"Yes." Eveline stroked Robyn's shorn hair. "There is the family we are born into. And also the family we choose."

Laurel floated into Robyn's mind again. Was she in prison? Was she alive? Had she been hurt?

Merryan, who like Robyn, like all of them, had lost her own parents. And she had been willing to give up the one shred of family she had left, her uncle. Merryan had been caught helping them. Had Crown punished her, too?

Even Scarlet. They could bicker about anything, it seemed, but they'd risked it all for each other time and again. Was this what it was like to have sisters?

"So you're kind of like my grandma, I guess," Robyn said. "Was she very beautiful, like you?"

"*Ach*," Eveline scoffed. "Do not let the eyes speak when it is the heart that tells the better story."

There she went, being all cryptic again. "Appearance doesn't matter?" Robyn deciphered the fortune-cookie phrasing. "I know that."

She pulled her beret back on, with the braid sewn into the back. Eveline smiled at the more familiar sight. Robyn pointed at her pleased expression. "But see, people still look first, and they want to like what they see."

"Ah, but the ones who truly know you will like what they see because they're seeing *you*," Eveline reached for

Robyn and hugged her. Over her shoulder, Robyn caught sight of herself in the bedside table's mirror. She might have inherited this special braid, but it had been all too easy to remove. Now, it was part of a costume. The hoodlum Robyn was pretending to be.

What if she was only pretending to be someone with a destiny?

≪CHAPTER TWENTY≫

Paint the Town

Key and Scarlet made their way back toward the cathedral. They would pick up their paint cans, then split up to proceed with the graffiti plan.

"That was good work, I guess," Key said. "But maybe not public enough. No one knows we stole the guns."

"A private slap in the face to the MPs can't hurt," Scarlet said. "Anyway, they'll know once they find Robyn's note." The girls had left their signature green sticky-note message on the side of the now-empty container.

They slipped inside through the plywood-covered door.

"Yeah, I meant that the general people don't know," Key said. "They should know we're building an arsenal. We should start getting them excited."

"The graffiti will get them excited. It gives them a quiet way to get involved."

"I know," Key said. "I just think we could do more."

"Anyway, a bunch of empty guns isn't exactly an arsenal," Scarlet said. "We're a long way from a street war."

"Did any of them even still have bullets?" Key asked casually.

"A couple," Scarlet said. "I emptied them." She pulled the small handful of bullets out of her pocket and poured them into an open desk drawer. She pushed it shut.

Key studied her actions thoughtfully.

Scarlet perched on the edge of the desk, balancing her feet on the edge of his chair. "How come you want a fight so bad anyway? You don't seem like the type."

Key's gaze flicked up to meet hers. "I plan ahead," he reminded her. "Like a chess game."

$$\ggg\!\longrightarrow$$

Everything seemed calm and normal outside of the Sherwood Health Clinic. Robyn watched from around the corner, studying the comings and goings of people through the main entrance. Any minute now, Merryan should arrive to volunteer.

After what happened this weekend, her uncle might be watching her. She probably wouldn't be able to get away to go to the cathedral. Robyn needed to know she was okay. That Crown hadn't thrown her in some dungeon along with Laurel and Tucker. Merryan had said she could handle her uncle, but really, who could handle Crown? Robyn doubted that the kind of man who would take over a government and threaten people's lives had a warm and fuzzy side.

She waited for over an hour. No sign of her friend. Maybe she had gone in some special side entrance.

It seemed safe enough for the time being, so Robyn strolled across the street and into the clinic lobby. She walked up to the check-in desk and greeted the nurse on duty.

"I'm a friend of Merryan Crown's," she said. "I know she's busy working right now but I'd really like to say hello, if I could."

"Oh, I'm sorry," said the desk nurse. "I'm afraid she couldn't make it to her volunteer shift today." The nurse looked saddened suddenly. "We do hope she'll be back here with us at some point. She really is a lovely girl."

"Thanks," Robyn said dejectedly. She hurried out of the building before anyone could recognize her.

This was bad. Very bad. Merryan wouldn't miss a day of work. Especially not today, of all days. What had Crown really done to her?

In a flurry of concern and desperation, Robyn pulled out her TexTer. Quickly she typed her message:

NEED TO KNOW. M OK?

≪CHAPTER TWENTY-ONE≫

A Familiar Tune

Key's small satchel rattled suspiciously. He tried to walk at a leisurely pace, but it was hard when he constantly wanted to duck out of sight as soon as possible. He painted arrow after arrow, on every brick wall, on every whitewashed fence. Bright green symbols of resistance, posted for the world to see.

He worked his way up and down the streets of Getty neighborhood, where the walls were short and the houses small and run-down. Getty was close to the heart of the resistance. Hardships had made the people strong. It had made them fighters.

People saw him working. He didn't try to hide. No one questioned him. "For Robyn," he would say, if anyone looked briefly puzzled.

Key tagged another fence, then tucked away his spray can. He didn't have to hide from the people, but he did have to worry about MPs appearing.

"*Gather the Elements as you will: Earth to ground you, Water to fill.*" The sound of a woman's singing caught his attention.

He followed the voice. He couldn't help it. The familiarity of the sound pulled him closer. It couldn't be, and yet . . .

"*Air to sustain, a Fire to ignite; Elements gather, all to fight.*"

The singer was a young woman in the backyard hanging up the wash. Key did not know her, and his heart sank a little. Of course, he shouldn't have been disappointed. It couldn't have been his mother. She was dead.

Not his first mother, he reminded himself, but his true mother—the woman who raised him. The one who had chosen and loved him when he was cast aside.

His first mother was also dead, he knew. But knowing that filled him with anger rather than sorrow.

His true mother had kept the knowledge from him as long as she could. He knew he was not born of her all along; her dark complexion against his paleness made that obvious. But she had tried to protect him from the truth of how unwanted he had been by everyone but her.

He was officially a person who didn't exist. His mother had saved him from certain death and raised him as her own. She had sacrificed for him, struggled with him.

"Gather the Elements as you will, till Earth cannot shake us, nor Water be still . . ."

As the words floated around him, it was impossible not to be reminded. How generous she was. How whole-heartedly rebellious.

He had repaid her gift by running. He hadn't been there when—

Key shook his head to clear his thoughts. The devastation of the Night of Shadows had cut deep across Sherwood. Someone like Robyn could be told the facts of that day, but she didn't really understand. Yes, her parents might have been better known than others, but they weren't the only ones who had disappeared.

"Air, boundless, our everything; the Fire, our true light; Elements gather, all to fight."

Key's quiet approach became less quiet when he bumped into a parked lawn mower.

The young woman flinched, interrupting the music. "Oh, you startled me," she said, clutching the clothes to her chest.

"You're singing," Key said. "It was a familiar song. That's all."

"A song of the resistance," the young woman said. "It keeps me calm, and it helps him sleep."

Key followed her gaze to the laundry basket at her feet. A chubby baby was curled up napping among the folded sheets.

"He's cute," Key said. *Moms liked to hear things like that*, he thought.

"The music was always important," she said. "I grew up hearing it."

"Me, too," Key said.

"They can put walls around us, but they can't erase our voices," the young woman said. She clipped articles of small clothing to the line. Little shirts and little undies all in a row, looking clean and damp. "Not many people sing anymore," she said. "But I still remember all the words."

"Let's teach everyone the words," Key said. "Make them remember."

$$\ggg\longrightarrow$$

"They've stolen what?" Mallet repeated. This was not good. Crown's seventy-two-hour timetable seemed more and more foolish as the hours ticked past. The hoodlum was still working her magic around Sherwood.

"The discarded weapons from the scrap metal facility," her aide reported.

Mallet fumed quietly. Discarding the weapons had been Shiffley's idea. She would have rather kept them for the upcoming ranks of trainees. Replacing them had been worth the expense in the long run, but the old guns were functional. Roll the new ones out in waves, as the old guns wore out, she'd suggested. But no. The new guns were bigger, sleeker, fancier, and certainly more imposing to anyone who might find him or herself on the business end of one. And Shiffley and Crown cared a great deal about appearances.

She pulled her own service weapon from her hip and studied it. They had perfectly good weapons for the senior MPs.

"We're still not sure how she got them out of the building," the aide said. "You'd need a forklift to budge that crate, and it's still here."

"Carried them out, perhaps?" Mallet mused. "The guns themselves are small, never mind the crate they were in."

"Oh," said the aide. "I suppose."

"Our weapons are upgraded," Mallet said. "We haven't lost much. Thank you for the report." She disconnected.

Mallet's fingertips tapped the desk. Her next call should be to the governor, or Shiffley. They would want to know that the hoodlum was arming herself. But the weapons were stolen from Sherwood. Instead of seeing it as a threat, Crown would no doubt see it as another failure by Mallet.

She did not pick up the phone.

≪CHAPTER TWENTY-TWO≫

Context Clues

As soon as it was close to dark, Robyn found Bridger waiting in the shadows beneath the statue in Sherwood Park, as they had planned. The plan was for her to lead him to the place where she'd hidden his belongings. Then they would both continue painting walls into the night. But now Robyn had an additional agenda—to find out what else he knew about the moon shrines.

"This would've been easier in the daylight," she told him, as they picked their way carefully through the alleys toward the hiding place.

"Can't show my face around Sherwood like that," Bridger grunted. "I'm a wanted fugitive, remember?"

"Well, if I could lift this thing on my own, I'd have brought it to you," Robyn said. The pack was so huge, it had taken both her and Laurel together to hide it successfully.

"Not a problem, girlie. I'm indebted to you for holding it."

Robyn grinned. "Good. I know how you're going to repay me."

Bridger didn't need any further prompting. "Look, you wanna have a conversation about the moon lore? There's not too much I can tell ya."

They arrived at the spot. Robyn pointed at the sewer grate, with the rope tied to its bars. "Here it is."

Bridger made a face. "You think I'm going down there? You must be crazy."

Robyn used a pipe to lever up the sewer grate far enough for Bridger to grasp it with his hands. "Grab and pull," she told him. He looked skeptical, but he took hold of the lip of the grate and eased it upward.

"Heavy," he grunted.

"Don't complain to me." Robyn laughed. "It's your own stuff."

As the grate came up, the rope came with it, bringing up the large backpack that had been dangling from it.

Bridger chuckled. "That's clever. I'm gonna remember that." He grabbed the rope with one strong hand and hauled the bag up to the surface. Robyn helped ease it out of the hole and onto the street.

"Now, let's see what we can do here." Bridger dug into the pack and extracted a few objects.

"We ate the food," Robyn admitted. "Call it a finder's fee."

Bridger shrugged. "It'd be bad by now, anyway. Good it got to some use." He pulled out a small circular box. Robyn remembered seeing it before, when they had hidden the pack. Bridger extracted a larger scrap of silver cloth from beneath the container. And a short dark wooden stick, from another side pouch. He handed them all to her. "Here. I've been chasing these down for years. Nothing come of it so far. Maybe you'll have better luck."

"What does it all mean?" she asked.

"I don't know," Bridger said. "I can't make sense of it. I'm smart enough, I guess, but maybe I don't have that kind of mind, for puzzle solving."

"Thanks." Robyn took the items, and tried to conceal her disappointment. More clues. No answers.

The stick was strangely rough to the touch, though it appeared smooth and round to her eye. The cloth, she stuck in her pocket. The round box was as tough to open as ever.

"No," Bridger said, "to open it you have to—"

"You there!" came a shout from the end of the alley.

"Fool," Bridger scolded himself. Robyn knew what he was thinking. They'd stayed out in the open too long. They should've returned to the cathedral immediately.

She leaped to her feet as a pair of MPs charged into the alley toward them.

"Get out of here," Bridger said. His pack listed to the side as he stood to face the MPs.

Robyn fumbled with the pack, trying to right it.

"You've got the goods. Run!" Bridger ordered. He took up the long pipe she'd used to pry the grate open. Wielding it like a bo, he advanced on the cops.

"Run," Bridger cried. He dodged and danced in front of the MPs. Robyn clutched the moon lore scraps and fled.

She stopped and looked back. Bridger flailed the pipe at the MPs, who now had guns drawn. He struck at one, but the other ducked around and took him in a choke hold from behind. Bridger wrestled as he went down.

Robyn stared in horror as the MPs bent over him. Bridger caught her eye. "Go!"

She hesitated, though she knew she shouldn't. Sacrifice was always going to be necessary.

"I've given you all I have," Bridger shouted. "The arrow is the key!"

If he said anything after that, she didn't hear it. She simply ran, breathless, in a zigzag formation back toward the safety of Nottingham Cathedral.

The arrow is the key. The map? She knew that much already. But there had to be more.

Robyn ran as fast as she could, ignoring the tightness in her chest and the twinge behind her eyes. How much longer did it have to be like this? How much more sacrifice did they all have to endure? The clock tower chimed ten p.m. Fifty-six hours until Crown's deadline.

Time to paint the town.

≪CHAPTER TWENTY-THREE≫

Resigned

Merryan Crown paced her bedroom suite. She could crawl out a window and make for Sherwood.

On foot.

In the dark.

By herself.

She ran a hand through her bobbed hair.

No, it was probably something she'd have to wait to do come morning. There were guards outside her door. There were guards beneath her window. *Your safety is paramount*, her uncle had said. But was it really her safety he was worried about?

Merryan knew that he didn't quite believe she was as innocent as she had pretended to be. Yes, she had let Robyn and her friends into the governor's mansion. Yes, she had helped the rebellion that was trying to take her uncle down.

Yes, she was a traitor . . . technically. And yet . . .

Merryan went to the window. She leaned against the edge of the sill and gazed out into the night. Her window faced the general direction of Sherwood. In the shadows she could see the treetops of the Notting Wood, and beyond that, the dark sky that hung over Sherwood.

She had betrayed her uncle. The only family she had left. And yet, somehow, it didn't feel wrong.

Could she continue to help Robyn's movement from within these walls?

She was safe here, as Uncle Iggy kept saying.

But this protected place, high on the hill, now felt like a prison of sorts. Within these walls, anything could happen. If her uncle made it such that she could never leave again, no one would miss her. No one would ever know.

$\ggg\!\!\longrightarrow$

Robyn deposited the round box, stick, and curtain scraps on Tucker's study table. Then she went and leaned against the door to the moon shrine. She reminded herself that it didn't matter that she couldn't get in. She recited the moon curtain verse to herself, like a lullaby.

She tried to remember that she wasn't as alone as she felt. Wherever they were in body, her friends were with her in spirit. Merryan, Tucker, Laurel. Robyn hoped hard for their safety. Key and Scarlet were already boldly proceeding with tonight's plan. Robyn needed to get moving, too.

She didn't know what to make of the new pieces that Bridger had given her, just that she had to take the cloth scraps out into the moonlight to try to read them. And that it was probably all he would ever give her. Another sacrifice. Another person who gave himself up so that she could keep going. What kind of world was this? What if she wasn't able to handle the responsibility when the next big moment came?

Robyn wondered again about Merryan, trapped in the governor's mansion. Possibly in more trouble than any of them knew. Merryan knew what it meant to make sacrifices. She had chosen the community over her own family, more than once. Why couldn't Robyn bring herself to do the same?

Was it as simple as the fact that Merryan's uncle was bad, and her own parents were good? Or was it more like Merryan was stronger than Robyn could ever hope to be?

There were six scraps of cloth now. She laid them out before her. They didn't appear to fit together in any particular pattern. Whatever fit in between them was still missing. An incomplete puzzle.

It was not even a high moon night. She'd have to wait until much later, after midnight to try to get a clear patch of moonlight. And by then, she'd be busy painting arrows all over town. If only she could get into the shrine, she'd be able to see the cloths in the moonlight without risking being seen.

Problems on top of problems. Robyn pushed away from the door and sighed. She shoved the scraps into her pocket and headed for the office to fill a satchel with paint.

I've given you all I have, Bridger had said.

But not all I need.

≪CHAPTER TWENTY-FOUR≫

Over the Airwaves

The imprisoned men huddled in their tents after the work lights came down for the night.

Tucker peered out the open flap at the darkened compound. Everything was still. Beyond the mounds of gravel stood the high barbed-wire fence. "Did you ever think about trying to get away?"

"It's too well guarded," Robert assured him. "We've looked into it."

Tucker knew a thing or two about scaling barbed-wire fences. It was possible. Robyn did it pretty regularly.

"Come back in here," Robert warned him. "You could be beaten for even the appearance of what you're talking about."

"I suppose," Tucker agreed. He let the tent flap fall back into place. Of course they would have tried. For him it had been hours behind the fence, but for them it was months.

Tucker was by nature a cautious and studious young man. The depth of his desire to buck the mold and escape from this enclosure surprised him. He was supposed to be a man of faith. Someone who took the hits life sent at him with determination, with patience. But that fence seemed so close, and so thin. For that to be the only barrier between these men and freedom—that hurt worse than brick walls and cell bars. An impenetrable dungeon.

Tucker shook his head. Clearly he had been spending too much time with the young hoodlums of his acquaintance.

And clearly Crown knew what he was doing, messing with the minds of his prisoners.

Tucker sat among the small group of men.

"Talk to us about what's going on out there," another man said. "We don't hear much."

"Yeah, the guards are tight lipped, even for cops."

"Well, the MPs . . . ," Tucker began.

"MPs?"

Tucker rewound his mind to the Night of Shadows, three months ago. The night they were taken prisoner. These men knew nothing about the state of the rebellion. It had been a fledgling thing at the time, with wings made of whispers. Now the movement had taken flight.

Tucker glanced at Robert. Robert, who had dropped his shovel upon learning the name of the leader of the rebellion. They had not been able to speak further at that moment. A guard had appeared and urged them to hurry. After that, the scrape of the shovels and the skitter of poured gravel filled the air, instead of words.

Tucker had sensed the conversation would continue overnight. He was right.

As the conversation among the men split and settled, Robert leaned toward Tucker. "Tell me about the girl. Robyn?"

Robert's face was drawn and pale. His hands lay slack at his sides.

"Yes," Tucker whispered. "The figurehead of the Crescendo is a twelve-year-old girl."

"How did this happen?" Robert mused, almost to himself.

"Perhaps it is written," Tucker answered carefully. "Perhaps only the shadows know. Why?" he added, curious as to the man's strong reaction.

Robert glanced at the others, who were engaged in their own conversations and did not appear to be listening. "Nothing. No reason."

Tucker could guess the reason, but he didn't. He sat alongside Robert, allowing silence to settle over them. Some things might be dangerous to speak aloud.

Tucker chose his words carefully. "Crown replaced the police force with a ramped-up version of security. Everything is locked down." He looked toward the tent flap, as if he could see the barbed-wire fence beyond it.

"Even outside of prison, it feels kinda like prison, you know?"

"Is it . . . ?" The men began peppering Tucker with questions about the new world order. He answered them all as best he could. Robert remained mostly quiet during the discussion, until the very end, when everyone was getting tired, and preparing for sleep.

"It sounds pretty bad out there," one of the men said.

"The world can be exceedingly cold," Robert responded. "And Crown wants everyone to know it."

$$\ggg\!\!\longrightarrow$$

In the dim quiet of the cathedral Nessa Croft set up her radio broadcast equipment. She watched the fingers on her analog watch tick toward the appointed hour. She tuned to the particular frequency and leaned into the mic.

"Good evening, Sherwood rebels. Coming out to you tonight from the deep deep reaches of our fair county."

She tipped her voice to someplace near a whisper. Quiet but steady, breathy but strong. Soothing as a bedtime story.

"I stand with Robyn. Will you stand with her, too? If you're listening tonight, you already know the world is not as it should be.

"Robyn's vision is of a Sherwood that is safe and livable for all. I've been fortunate enough to meet this remarkable young woman. I've looked into those eyes, and seen the strength there. She has come for us, and she will lead us toward the Sherwood we all deserve.

"No single person deserves the power Crown holds right now. Not power grasped through violence, wrenched from the hands of those elected by the people. Robyn's power comes *from* the people. A power that is rightful. That is earned. A power that *never* stands alone.

"Make no mistake, friends, Robyn's eyes hold the weight of the world. Our world. We cannot let her down. We cannot let her stand alone.

"I stand with Robyn. Will you stand with her, too? Crown will know our wrath. Crown will feel our rain. The storm is coming."

≪CHAPTER TWENTY-FIVE≫

Static

"The storm is coming," said the woman's sultry voice. It felt like the kind of promise anyone listening would want kept.

Bill Pillsbury clicked the recording off, and looked toward his boss. Governor Crown stroked his thin mustache and glared at the device as though the woman speaking was actually inside it.

"From where do they broadcast? Surely you can follow the signal," the governor said.

"Well, not really. The broadcasts are short. We've intercepted a few, but not in time to trace the signal before it's gone."

The governor's brows folded into a V. "I'm given to understand that anything sent over the WebNet is traceable, even after the fact. There are signatures."

"Unfortunately, they're not using the WebNet. They're using actual radio. Not digital broadcasting.

These are not replayable podcasts. It is much lower tech. One and done."

Crown looked thoughtful.

"We might be able to track a live signal, but they change frequencies and timing of broadcasts. They're even operating in code."

"Crack their code."

"We're working on it," Pillsbury assured him. Still, the governor did not look satisfied. "I could have the tech staff come up and explain it a bit better," he offered. "As your press secretary, I'm mostly concerned with the likely impact—"

Crown cut him off. "Technology serves a function. Progress. Advancement." He stroked his mustache. "They can't operate in the real world, because I control that world."

"That's true, sir. However, that doesn't mean we can dismiss—"

Crown waved his hand. "Their pitiful efforts will die, just like the outmoded technology they're using."

Pillsbury felt himself being dismissed. The governor's attentions were rapidly turning to other things. "Sir, I must impress upon you the power of this method as an organizing strategy."

Crown said nothing.

"The tone of the broadcasts promises significant unrest," Pillsbury explained. "We have reason to believe that the citizens of Sherwood are planning some sort of uprising."

Crown leaned back in his chair, clearly annoyed to have to keep talking about this topic. "The girl, Robyn. Is it her voice on the broadcast?"

"No, but she's referred to. Shall I play the excerpt for you again?"

Nessa Croft's throaty alto filled the room. "Crown will feel our rain. The storm is coming."

"That won't be necessary," Crown spoke over the voice. "Unless you're saying you are unequipped to take care of this minor inconvenience for me."

Pillsbury stopped the recording. In the wake of the sultry-sounding threats, the silence deafened.

"I can take care of the radio problem," he said confidently. "We can try jamming their frequencies and things like that. It needn't occupy any more of your time." Pill pocketed the recording and headed toward the door. Over his shoulder he offered a final piece of advice.

"You might consider a more diplomatic approach to the Robyn situation. They have the power of numbers. We may not be best served by strong-arming our way through this."

"I am in charge here," Crown said. "They'll yield to me soon enough." He waved his hand at the recording device. "Lip service."

Pill nodded thoughtfully. "The real problem isn't the broadcast itself, you understand. It's the question of who might be listening and ready to respond. It's the conviction with which she promises the storm."

The door closed firmly behind Pillsbury, leaving Crown alone with his thoughts.

$$\ggg\longrightarrow$$

Mallet also listened to the pirate radio broadcast recording. When it finished, she braced herself for the call she was going to have to make.

It was time to show Crown she was one step ahead of him. Like always.

"I've determined the identity of the girl," she reported. Crown didn't need to know that she'd been sitting on the information for several days. "Her name is Robyn Loxley, age twelve. Daughter of—"

"Robert Loxley, of Parliament."

Mallet's heart skipped. "Yes, that's correct."

There was a long silence.

"You wanted the name," Mallet said finally. "And I've delivered. Now I'd like to discuss—"

"This girl was to be brought in on the first night," Crown reminded her. As if Mallet could ever forget. "Your failure is compounded."

Mallet said nothing. She knew this to be true.

"Your services are not needed at this time," Crown continued.

Mallet fumed silently. If they knew the rebels were arming themselves, they wouldn't be so quick to ignore her. "We really should consider—"

Crown cut her off. "Sherwood seems about all you can handle."

"We will catch the hoodlum," Mallet promised.

"*I* will catch the hoodlum," Crown thundered. "You have failed."

The line went dead.

$$\gg\!\!\!\longrightarrow$$

Crown rammed his fist into the End Call button on his screen. He missed the days when you held a phone in your hand and could slam it onto a table or throw it across the room.

Robert Loxley, the insufferable defender of Sherwood County. Of course his daughter would turn out to be the troublemaking girl. It would bring Crown a great deal of pleasure to see Loxley's head in a vise.

$$\gg\!\!\!\longrightarrow$$

Mallet sat still and listened to the vacuum sound of disconnect. It filled her office. It filled her mind. It tried to make its way into her heart, but the door was already closed. She would not let Ignomus's insults get to her. Not anymore.

Crown was a fool if he didn't take the threats against him seriously. If he thought that Robyn's success was indicative of Mallet's incompetence.

How short-sighted could he be? How drunk on power, to imagine himself so infallible?

Did he not realize what effort had gone in to putting him in the governor's chair? What she had sacrificed on his behalf?

Soon he would realize her true power. And then he would be the one forced to bow and scrape and beg.

Mallet stormed out of her office and took to the elevators.

》》—→

The underlings quivered when Mallet walked in. The head lab tech sensed their discomfort and stopped doling out instructions. He turned toward the door. "Hello, Sheriff."

"A word?" she said. Her gaze flicked over the room.

The tech signaled a "wait" motion to his staff and stepped toward the sheriff.

The lab tech hesitated. "Sheriff," he said finally. "You do realize you could message these tasks to me."

"Yes," she said. "I prefer there not be a record of the request." She showed him the list of library books. "I need to know who checked these out."

The tech nodded. "So be it."

"Thank you," she said. "I do appreciate your efforts."

As she strode out of the room, she swore the men in the room sat a little taller. See? How hard was that? To show a little appreciation for those who helped you get the job done.

In the elevator, Mallet reflected on her own situation. It would be nice, wouldn't it, to hear for once that she was doing something right in Sherwood.

The fact was, apart from the nuisance of the hoodlum, she was taking care of business in a major way. Who else could have rallied the MPs to lock down Sherwood and Block Six in this short window of time?

She pulled her shoulders back. That's right. She was killing it in Sherwood. Crown should be able to see her for what she was. But he couldn't.

He wasn't seeing her. He wasn't even looking anymore.

Mallet's throat tightened. All of these efforts to prove herself to him, and he wasn't even looking. All he could see, all he wanted to see, was her flaws.

Well. When the time was right, she'd show him. She'd show him it was a mistake to underestimate Marissa Mallet.

≪CHAPTER TWENTY-SIX≫

No Road Map

Laurel knelt beside the fountain in the park, clutching the biggest tube of toothpaste she had ever owned. It was almost as long as her forearm. She cradled it there, like a baby.

The toothbrush was also special. It had different colored bristles of different lengths. They fanned out to touch more parts of your tooth at once.

She rinsed the brush under the flowing water, then tucked it carefully back into her new bag.

Laurel knew one thing for certain: life in the Castle District would be easy. It was scary here, because she didn't know where she was, but in a bigger way, it wasn't scary AT ALL here. There were no MPs to hide from, no checkpoints making her fear being caught or questioned. They had very comfortable parks. And big fancy stores full of people who wouldn't notice the cost of an extra item or two in their shopping basket. Stores so big and so fancy, she didn't even need to borrow things from them. She could just stay inside. She could have dinner every night, up on top of the shelves in aisle 24. It would be magical.

But it would be lonely.

All her new friends were far away. Sleeping in the store had been easy enough, but waking up and knowing there wasn't anyone nearby to watch her back? That was harder than she'd expected.

Laurel had always managed on her own. She didn't even remember ever having a family. She must've had one, a long time ago. Before she was able to fend for herself. Someone had fed her bottles and changed her diapers and rocked her to sleep. But all she remembered was orphanages and homes, snippets of memory that took the shape of crib bars and institutional sheets with company names stamped across them in brown or gray ink. White walls and windows that didn't open, and other kids clambering to share the small pool of toys.

She had run away as soon as she figured out it was possible. The streets of Sherwood became her home. They still were, she reminded herself. Everything she had now was temporary. It was always going to disappear. Someday.

The thought twisted up inside her and made her reach for the toothbrush again. She held it in her hand, thinking.

It had only been three months, but it seemed she had gotten used to having other people close by her. She had gotten used to waking up in the same bed morning after morning, even if it was an old mattress on the floor. She had colorful sheets now, ones she had picked out herself on one of the crew's supply runs. They were orange, dotted with small paintbrushes spilling out rainbows. There was no such thing as toothbrush sheets, apparently, but these had been close enough to delight her.

She missed those sheets. As the sun sank over the city, she wanted nothing more than to curl up in them. It was scary, to feel attached to something that lived in one place. Normally, she kept stashes of her stuff all over Sherwood. But in the last few weeks, the Nottingham Cathedral had become something she counted on. A place to think of as home.

》》⟶

It had been twenty-four hours already. The seventy-two-hour deadline loomed large in Robyn's mind. Now it was only forty-eight. And she was no closer to a solution. Not from the Crescendo, and not from the moon lore.

She turned Bridger's round box over in her hands. There was something important inside it, she was sure. Dripping a little oil on the hinges hadn't helped. The clasp was fixed fast. It had a little keyhole in it, not even big enough for her pinky finger.

"Tonight is going to be great," Scarlet said. "Did you hear the broadcast? Nessa made you sound like some kind of goddess." Her usually wry voice took on a tone of awe.

"Nessa's voice would make anything sound good," Robyn murmured. She knew she was no kind of goddess. Far from it.

Key bounded into the room. "We got a text back." He read it aloud. "M OK FOR NOW."

"For now?" Robyn echoed. She allowed herself to feel relief at the knowledge that Merryan was safe. Texts from Pillsbury were few and far between, but usually carried important information.

"What else should we ask him?" Key wondered. "It's maddening, how little he'll say."

"He doesn't want to get caught," Scarlet said.

"How would he get caught?" Key argued. "This thing is so old. That's why we can use it at all."

"He probably doesn't know that much," Robyn suggested. But she did wonder. Did he know where her parents were being held? Did he know how, when, and where Crown planned to kill them? "Try asking for prisoner information."

"WHERE IS IT BEING HELD?" Key typed. As press secretary, Pill would have heard Crown's threat. He would know "it" meant Robyn's parents.

They all stared at the TexTer for a few moments.

"It could take hours for him to respond," Scarlet said, spinning back toward her monitors. "I have work to do."

Robyn and Key didn't move for a while. "We're all worried about her," Key said finally. "About all of them."

"That's not what I was thinking about," Robyn lied. "I was just trying to imagine what will happen in forty-eight hours. If we don't—If we can't—"

Key gazed at her sternly. "You're not turning yourself in. What would even come of that? He hasn't promised us he'll release them. We'd just end up with all of you behind bars. No one wants that."

"I'm not turning myself in," Robyn agreed. "My parents would want me to keep fighting for everyone, not just for them. But every minute we waste, they're running out of time."

"The plan is good," Key said. "We show them that 'Robyn' is more than one girl. You're an idea that everyone in Sherwood will stand behind. If he hurts your parents, we only make things worse for him. That'll be clear after tonight."

Robyn nodded. It had sounded like a good idea yesterday. It *was* a good idea, she insisted to herself. But Crown didn't seem likely to give up his threat against her parents that easily.

The seconds kept ticking by. *I'm running out of time.*

≺CHAPTER TWENTY-SEVEN≻

A Message on the Books

The MP lab boys came through, as usual. The moon lore library books had been checked out by a seminary student named Tucker Branch.

Mallet sat behind her console and typed his name into the search field. When his profile came up she smiled.

The system showed he was a student at the nearby seminary. A man of the cloth. Or, at least, potentially. That made him honor bound to respect law and order, she supposed.

She scrolled down. A red flag popped up at the edge of the screen: INCARCERATED.

Well, well, look at this.

It wouldn't matter if Tucker wanted to cooperate. He was already in the system. He would cooperate. And his books could be confiscated as part of whatever investigation was underway.

Mallet punched a button on the console. "Coming down to the car. Warm up the engine."

"Yes, Sheriff," her assistant responded.

Minutes later, Mallet's motorcade streamed east on the Cannonway, toward the seminary.

Tucker Branch was a lazy housekeeper. His dorm room, which was barely the size of a walk-in closet, was covered with a thin layer of lived-in clutter. Socks and T-shirts and undershorts, newspapers and term papers and cereal boxes—most of his few belongings appeared strewn about in plain sight. There was a narrow, unmade bed, and a small desk with piles of homework and a used coffee mug on it.

Few books of any kind. No sign of any computer or tablet. Either Tucker Branch was a terrible student, or he was doing his studying someplace else.

Mallet pulled up his prisoner record. Arrested . . . in conjunction with— *Well, well.* Things just got more and more interesting. Time to have a little chat with Tucker Branch.

$$\text{\textbf{≫}}\longrightarrow$$

Merryan retreated to her room immediately after school. There was no point in trying to get out of the house today, either. Guards at her door and under her window. She was trapped.

She clicked into her messages, hoping maybe Scarlet had found a way to reach out to her through normal channels. It should be possible. In fact, it was frustrating that the others hadn't thought to try to contact her. Didn't they care at all?

She opened a message from the administrative director of the Sherwood clinic:

> We're so sorry to hear that you won't be able to volunteer anymore. You've been such a help around the clinic. Please do stop by and visit us, when you have a chance! We'd love to have a moment to say good-bye and thank you for your hard work.

Merryan leaped out of her desk chair and pounded out of the room, startling the guard stationed in her hallway.

"Uh, Miss Crown? Is everything—" Clearly everything was not all right. He swept along after her as she stomped her way toward the governor's office.

"Oh, hello, Merryan—" Her uncle's assistant got about halfway through the greeting before Merryan had blown past her.

She wrenched open the door to her uncle's office. He was sitting behind the desk, perusing a stack of important-looking papers.

"HOW LONG?" she demanded. "HOW LONG ARE YOU GOING TO KEEP ME TRAPPED IN HERE?"

Crown furrowed his brow. "Trapped? I think that's an over—"

"Trapped," Merryan insisted, rudely speaking over him. Something she would never have dreamed of doing a matter of days ago. "You told my volunteer job I was quitting? Without even asking me? You have guards outside my door. I feel trapped."

"The guards are there for your protection. We had a breach, you understand."

"Are you going to blame me for that forever?" she cried.

"I don't blame you."

"I made one mistake. The mistake of trusting people. And thinking that they liked me for who I am." Her eyes welled up. The real sorrow over not being able to connect with her new friends took over. "The truth is, I liked them. I thought we were going to be . . . something." She pushed away the fresh bout of tears and crossed her arms. "But I screwed up. And now you're punishing me. So, how long?"

"I won't respond if you continue to raise your voice to me," Crown said coolly. "If we can speak in rational tones, we can have this conversation."

"This isn't a conversation," Merryan shouted. "This is a FIGHT."

"I will not—"

"People fight!" Merryan continued. "Families. When other people do something that hurts them. Like you, trying to take away everything I love." She knew she should dial it back, to avoid sending her uncle over the edge, but really, why should she act like everything was fine? Wouldn't that be weirder, under the circumstances?

Crown sat silent.

Merryan sucked in several breaths and tried to speak more calmly. "You want to know me? The real me? I'm someone who likes to help people."

"I know that about you already."

She swiped at her tears. "I'm best at helping. If you take that away, I have nothing."

"That's not true."

"You could help people, too," she cried. "But you don't want to."

Crown cleared his throat. "I want to help you," he said. "Look, there is a lot going on in Sherwood right now. I can't expect you to understand, but it's not safe for you there. At least for the next couple of days. We can revisit this conversation next week, when things are calmer all around."

"Next week?" Merryan echoed. "You promise?"

Crown sighed. "I promise. Everything will be better in a couple of days. Sherwood will be safe again soon."

Merryan breathed. That did not sound like good news for Robyn. "Thank you," she whispered, then stalked out of the governor's office.

Her shouting had apparently drawn a few bystanders. When she stepped out of the office, the assistant

and the press secretary, Bill Pillsbury, were both standing there.

"I was coming to see him," Pill told the assistant.
"But perhaps I'll give him a private moment or two . . ."
He scooted into the hallway, just behind Merryan as
she left.

"Try not to take it personally," Pill said, catching up
to her quickly with his long-legged gait.

"He really doesn't care about anyone," Merryan
blurted out, glancing over her shoulder. "How is that
possible?"

Pill sighed. "Your uncle is a complicated man."

"He's a tyrant."

Pill glanced up and down the hallway. He placed a
hand on Merryan's shoulder and eased her into a quiet
office.

"He does care about you, I'm sure."

Merryan shook her head. "Not about me. Not about
the city, the people—"

"*Shh*. It's best not to speak of some things."

Merryan blotted tears from her eyes.

Pill patted her shoulder awkwardly. "He's not been
the same since she died, you know."

"My dad used to say that, too," Merryan agreed.
"But this is the only way I've known him."

Pill studied the girl thoughtfully. "Perhaps you
remind him too much of what might have been. He was
quite looking forward to fatherhood, I think."

"Fatherhood?" Merryan echoed.

Pill's face folded into a frown. "Oh. I've let the cat out of the bag, have I?"

"I don't understand," Merryan said.

"Their child would have been about your age, I suppose. A boy, I think. Poor lad died with his mother."

This was news to Merryan. The story she knew was that her aunt had fallen ill, a couple of years before she was born. But really, she had died in childbirth?

"Anyway," Pill said. "Back to work. Keep your chin up, kiddo."

As she headed toward the door, his voice followed her. "Everyone is all right, including you."

She turned around. "What?"

"Everyone is all right," he said, gazing at her meaningfully. "That is to say, the important thing is just to be yourself. People will care about you for who you are. In fact, it'll be hard to stop them from caring." He smiled wryly. "You'll see, in time."

≪CHAPTER TWENTY-EIGHT≫

The Live Oaks

A commotion outside the tent startled Tucker awake. The other men shifted restlessly. They glanced at each other in fear.

"What's happening?" Tucker asked.

"It's better not to know," Robert answered. He moved toward Tucker's cot. "Stay behind me. It'll be okay."

Another man joined him, their bodies forming a wall in front of Tucker. Tucker fiddled with the corner of his thin blanket.

The tent flap parted and two MPs walked in. The one with the mustache seemed to be in charge. He looked around. "Where's the kid?" he demanded.

"I'm not a kid." Tucker stood up from behind the men. Robert shielded him with an arm as he tried to push between them.

"Nice try, Loxley," said the one with the mustache.

"Take me," Robert offered. "It ought to be my turn."

"Nah," said Mustache. "We have our orders. Anyway, the governor has something special planned for you. When the time is right."

"It's okay," Tucker said, even though he had never felt less okay about anything. The MPs seized him by the shoulders and led him outside.

"Stay strong!" Robert's voice followed him through the canvas.

"Where are you taking me?" Tucker asked.

"You don't know?" Mustache smiled coldly. "Why ruin the suspense?"

>>>———>

Laurel stood next to the fountain, feeling uncertain. Back home in Sherwood, there was no problem a good toothbrushing couldn't solve. It gave her time to think. And plan. By the time she was tossing the floss away, she usually knew what to try next.

This trick didn't work so well in Castle District. Laurel's teeth were clean, but she still had no idea which way to run.

She climbed to the top of the fountain, the highest thing around. Water flowed over her hands and feet, making the concrete slick. Balanced on her toes near the apex, she studied the view in all directions. City buildings poked up all around.

There was one crop of very tall, shiny buildings straight ahead of her. That must be the downtown part of Castle District. Behind her stood rows and rows of houses. Their rooftops arced upward, following the slight rise of the earth leading to the governor's mansion, shining gold atop its hill.

Laurel shivered. Well, at least now she knew which way NOT to run.

In the distance, to her left, sparkling water gleamed. To her right, leafy greenery stretched as far as her eye could see.

What had Robyn said about the map? Castle District had a lake on one side and a forest on the other. Laurel remembered that Robyn's big fancy house backed up against the woods. And on the other side of those woods would be Sherwood.

Laurel skidded down the fountain and splashed out of the pool. She picked up her backpack and scurried in the direction of the woods.

>>>——→

Laurel strolled the neighborhoods, combing up and down the streets. The houses were all big and fancy but seemed to get bigger and fancier the closer she got to the woods. Robyn's street, she remembered, had houses with gates and walls and fences. Those would be the houses closest to the woods, she figured.

Once she found the house, she could go through the woods behind it to get to Sherwood. The trail she'd followed with Robyn dumped out at Tent City. Exactly where Laurel wanted to be.

But it wasn't one long street of houses. It was all kinds of different small neighborhoods, broken up by patches of fancy shops and intersecting streets. The houses were far apart, too, with lawns as big as some school playgrounds in Sherwood.

Laurel paced along the winding roads until she found a place that felt familiar. A gated driveway. Glossy white bricks three stories high. The plaque on the gate had a big L followed by lots of other letters.

L *for Laurel*, she thought, satisfied. She began to scale the gate.

She peeked over the wall. An MP van was parked in the driveway. Lights were on in the house.

Laurel gulped. How could she have forgotten this inconvenient detail? Robyn's house had become an MP barracks. They'd had to hide from the MPs last time they were here. And Laurel knew, too, that there were cameras monitoring the driveway and all the entrances.

You can get out of anywhere if you're small, Laurel thought. Maybe you could also get *in* anywhere.

She swung her legs over the gate and beelined across the lush grass toward the tree line.

When she reached the relative safety of the woods, Laurel paused to catch her breath. The manor house seemed still. If any MPs had spotted her crossing, they gave no indication of it.

The sun had not set, but it would soon. Under the trees, everything was already cast in spooky shadows. Laurel inched her way deeper, because she had to, but her heart raced and she kept trying to open her eyes even wider.

She emerged into the small clearing at the ring of Live Oaks. The huge, sturdy trees felt familiar and safe. She had been here with Robyn, and that made it better.

The rest of the woods were too dark and scary alone at night. Daylight would be better. Laurel climbed the thick trunk of Robyn's favorite Live Oak, curled into a branch, and tried to sleep.

≪CHAPTER TWENTY-NINE≫

Interrogation

So much for flying under the radar, Tucker thought. He was staring at Marissa Mallet, sheriff of Sherwood.

The room was small and white, like a doctor's office but without the right furniture. It smelled musty, not at all like medicine, but Tucker had a suspicion he would be feeling some pain pretty soon. He rocked in place on his chair, testing its strength. His hands were bound behind him.

"You are in possession of some materials that interest me," Mallet said. She paced the room in front of him, menacingly calm.

"That seems unlikely." Tucker was confused. "I don't have anything you'd want."

"We've raided your home," Mallet said.

Tucker's brain flashed over the contents of his apartment. He could think of nothing related to the

Crescendo, or Robyn. "Then you've already seen everything I own," he said.

"I'm interested in your reading material. The books you checked out of the library."

Now Tucker was really confused. "For my dissertation?"

"Apparently." Mallet stalked closer. "Tell me about it."

Of all the surreal experiences . . . Tucker shook his head. Prison camp seemed more believable than this scenario. Why would the sheriff of Sherwood possibly care about his dissertation? His closest friends barely cared about his studies.

"I'm studying the origins of the moon lore," Tucker reported. He didn't see any harm in saying it.

"The teachings hold significance to your rebels, do they not?"

Oh. "Uh—" Tucker stammered.

"Where are the books?"

"If they're not in my apartment, it's because I've returned them."

"Try again," Mallet snapped. "Where are you keeping these documents?"

Tucker's skin prickled. He couldn't tell her. If he confessed, Robyn's hideout would be raided within minutes.

"I—I use a study carrel in the school library," he offered. "Some of them could be there?"

Mallet raised her PalmTab and typed something in. "Good. Where else?"

"Nowhere else. My apartment. The libraries . . . I don't know." He was a good liar, he thought. When the cause was good, and the pressure was on, he'd done okay in the past. But sitting under arrest, facing the sheriff, was something different. He could tell she was not convinced by his story.

"Understand." Mallet's voice dropped. "We have methods for . . . inspiring people to talk."

Tucker swallowed hard. "I don't have anything to say."

"Suit yourself." Mallet pounded out of the room. The door slamming open punctuated her exit. It did not close on its own.

Tucker looked into the void of a dimly lit hallway.

Mallet's voice floated back to him. "String him up," she told the guard. "No mercy. I want him singing a different tune after the showcase."

The guard said, "Yes, Sheriff." He reached in with an arm and swung the door shut.

Alone now, in the quiet white room, Tucker struggled to calm himself. He pushed all thoughts of Nottingham Cathedral deeper and deeper into himself, as if to forget such a place existed. He told himself a new story, one about an abandoned shed in the Heights. A quiet place, perfect for isolated study. He thought warm thoughts about how much he loved to go there.

He told himself the story over and over, trying to make it feel true. If they made him give up a story, he would only tell this lie.

Tucker drew deep meditative breaths. It would be okay. He was a doctoral candidate. He already knew a fair amount about withstanding torture.

$$\gg\!\!\!\longrightarrow$$

True to her uncle's word, the guard did not follow Merryan back to her room. This newfound freedom, which would have seemed totally normal a few days ago, made her think about where to go and what to do. She found herself wandering toward her uncle's room.

Merryan thought about their old house. She'd rarely been in her uncle's room there, either, but it had never felt truly forbidden. Not in the way this felt now.

She took a deep breath and eased the sliding doors open. His suite of rooms was quite a bit larger than hers. But much less lived-in. The only thing on the floor was a large woven rug and the legs of all the furniture. Otherwise, the room was very spare. Merryan scanned the neatly dusted surfaces of the oak dresser and coffee table. Barely a coaster. One small prescription bottle and a pair of reading glasses. But nothing to actually read.

The walk-in closet was lined with clean pressed suits in varying shades of black and gray.

The bathroom had been neatly wiped and cleaned, with fresh towels installed. The same thing happened to her bathroom while she was at school each day, but even that didn't end up so sterile. She had her rows of nail polish bottles on the counter, a dozen stray tubes of lip gloss, all kinds of lotions and things that smelled nice. Open a drawer, and hair ties would come springing out.

Here, there were empty drawers. A single bar of soap on a tray in the large, fancy shower. A razor and shaving foam in the cabinet over the sink. A toothbrush.

Merryan's heart felt heavy. There was no warmth in this suite. Nothing to indicate a person who enjoyed anything about life. No secret drawer of candy. No folded photo of his lost love.

Was her uncle so cold that he didn't keep a photo of his late wife in any room of the mansion? There wasn't one in his office, she knew, but not even in his own room?

They shared this large house, and yet they didn't know each other at all.

≪CHAPTER THIRTY≫

The Showcase

Tucker strained his neck, trying to find an angle through which he could see past the black cloth blindfold. His hands were bound, his feet were not—but making a run for it would be impossible while he couldn't see. He could dash off a cliff, or into traffic, or straight into the waiting arms of an MP who would make him pay for the moment of disobedience.

There was no wind, so it seemed unlikely that he was cliffside.

The whisper of traffic felt somewhat distant, the way it usually did in the deepest parts of Sherwood, far from the high-speed expressways that wound through Nott City. It was a vague brush of sound at the edge of his mind, noticeable only because he was listening for clues.

He began to hear sounds of people arriving. Snatches of voices growing closer, gathering. An ebb and flow of murmurs and silences. Not a joyful gathering. Something somber.

"Let's go." An MP nudged him to take a few steps. Tucker shuffled forward. His shin banged into something hard. "Climb," the MP barked. Tucker carefully lifted his feet and climbed a short flight of stairs. He found himself standing on some kind of makeshift platform. Wooden planks bowed under his feet as he moved.

"Right here," the MP said, placing a hand on Tucker's shoulder. He bent down and clipped shackles to Tucker's ankles. Metal cuffs that drew his legs apart such that he was forced to stand at ease. Not that he felt at ease. Quite the opposite.

The MP freed his hands from the ropes and clipped chains around his wrists as well. The cold metal pulled his arms wide like wings. Then the MP pulled the cloth off Tucker's eyes.

He immediately wanted the blindfold back. He had already sensed what was happening, but to see it made it worse somehow.

He was chained in an X formation, like the Vitruvian Man. Standing on a platform—a stage—in front of a gathering crowd.

"Welcome to the showcase," the MP told him. The gaze that fell upon Tucker's face was cold, but thoughtful. "Don't try to be strong. They want the crowd to know your pain. So the more you scream, the faster it'll be over."

》》》——→

The workers filed into the square. They moved slowly, to show their resignation, but not too slowly. After the long day's work, they all just wanted to go home.

The workers had long since grown weary of this exercise. Crown's weekly show of force, a reminder that they were all at his whim.

The space was ringed with MPs. Some stood on blocks, to better survey the crowd. Others nudged and corralled the workers into position. No one struggled. No one stepped out of line. The procession was smooth and routine.

The prisoner this week was young, far younger than any of the prisoners they had seen on display. Far younger than most of the workers themselves. This piqued their interest, briefly, before the worry and frustration settled back in.

Beneath the worry and frustration, a ripple of something else passed through the crowd. It was noticeable, but not quite palpable. Like a word caught on the tip of your tongue.

A ripple of anticipation. Excitement.

Because things would be different today, some of them knew.

The storm was coming.

⫷CHAPTER THIRTY-ONE⫸

The Storm

"It's recording," Scarlet said. She knelt beside her portable computer console while Robyn looked on.

"Yeah?"

"See for yourself."

The girls were crouched on the roof of a building nearby to the workers' showcase. They had decided it was too risky to try to get closer. Instead, they had hacked into the surveillance feed from nearby cameras.

Scarlet's console had four small screens, each displaying a different angle.

"How many cameras do you have going?" Robyn asked.

"I found ten cameras in the immediate area," Scarlet answered. "I was able to piggyback on six, but I'm having trouble keeping the last one." Her fingers flew over the keyboard. "I'm going to drop down to four. Less noticeable. More sustainable."

She wasn't really talking to Robyn anymore. "It's enough, I think. A couple good angles."

It was plenty.

Almost too much, really.

It was terrible, seeing Tucker up onstage, being punished for Robyn's actions. His head was bowed and his back arched with each strike of the strap against it. When he cried out from the pain, it was desperate prayers to the sky, to the moon and the shadows that bore him.

It went against her spirit, not to try to save him. But she breathed through the awful sinking feeling. Pushed away the knowledge that she had let him down. Tucker was filling a role that had to be filled. It would be just as awful to see anyone else in his place.

The images didn't stay long. Scarlet pecked and typed into black, flipping screens.

Robyn's heart skipped. "Is it gone?"

"No, I just . . ." Scarlet's voice trailed off. She was focused. Moments later she resurfaced to reassure Robyn. "It's still recording."

Robyn paced the rooftop behind her. "You're getting one of the stage, and several of the crowd?"

Scarlet nodded. "Front of stage, back of stage looking over the crowd, two wider angles on the square."

"Why haven't they started it? We have to get the actual thing on tape." Frustrated, she kicked at pebbles on the black tarred roof.

"If it happens," Scarlet said. "I'll get it."

Robyn stared at the screens. Tucker's cries.

It would happen. It had to.

》》⟶

Five minutes later, it happened.

The low sound started from somewhere in the crowd. They would never be able to determine where.

Clicking, shushing. The snapping of fingers, the rubbing of palms. Simple sounds, alone. Simple movements. But rising from the crowd together, the sounds formed a gently symphony. A noise like breeze through leaves, raindrops falling on roofs.

The MPs surrounding the square looked toward the sky, as if expecting to get wet. But the sky was clear.

"Those who wish to step out of line," yelled the man onstage. "All you dissidents, and would-be dissidents, hear me. Those who would stand with the hoodlum will pay the price."

The whip cracked down over Tucker.

"Never forget what will happen!" the MP shouted.

"We will never forget," said the crowd.

The MP's whip faltered. Usually the crowd stood silent.

The words rippled back and out, echoing over the square.

"We will never forget."

"We will never forget."

The sounds of rain intensified. The workers kept snapping fingers, rubbing palms, slapping their thighs, stomping their feet until the air filled with thunder, as if a real downpour was imminent.

"The storm is coming." The words rippled through the crowd. "The storm is coming."

"Stop them," the lead MP ordered.

The other MPs looked around, uncertain. The noise was coming from everywhere.

"Stop them!" he repeated. He shoved the two MPs nearest him into the crowd. But the workers nearest the edge stood firm and quiet. The rain came from within them. The rain could not be stopped.

The MPs pushed past the edges of the crowd, trying to get to the culprits at the center. In doing so, they found themselves surrounded.

"For Sherwood, unite," called a voice from somewhere.

"For Sherwood, we fight," the workers responded.

"Don't just stand there," the lead MP ordered. "Stop this!"

But they couldn't.

Fear grew in the eyes of the MPs. The terror that the few feel when the many begin to show hints of disobedience.

≪CHAPTER THIRTY-TWO≫

A Show of Force

The MPs tossed Tucker back into the tent, dropping a small package of medical supplies alongside him. The other men rushed forward to help him. In the lantern light, his wounds glowed red and gold. The men helped him ease onto the cot, and began cleaning the wounds with damp cloth. They had been ready for him. This was their weekly routine.

"These wounds look worse than usual," one man said.

Robert nodded as he tended to Tucker. "What happened?"

"I didn't cave," Tucker said. "I didn't give up any information."

The men exchanged glances. "Information?"

"Is he delirious?" another man whispered.

"It's supposed to be just a simple beating. To show that they hold all the power," said a third man.

"It wasn't just," Tucker whispered. "She wanted to know things that I know. She's going after Robyn."

Robert's face tightened. "The girl." He motioned the other men to step back, so only he and Tucker were speaking.

"What do you know about Robyn?"

Tucker shook his head, then winced in pain. "No. I won't tell you."

"It's safe to tell me," Robert insisted. "I would die before I let anything happen to Robyn."

"It was weird," Tucker said. "She must be trying every angle to find her."

"She?"

"The sheriff."

"You saw the sheriff?"

"She questioned me."

"Why would the sheriff question you?"

"I know things."

Robert acknowledged that with a nod. "I mean, why now? Why not on the way here? After they captured you."

"I won't let them find her," Tucker promised. He closed his eyes and let the pain overtake him. "I will never tell what I know."

$$\ggg\!\longrightarrow$$

The video recordings came through clean and crisp, better than Robyn had imagined.

First, they'd cut and spliced the feed from the different cameras to show the best angles.

"Editing is not my expertise," Scarlet muttered as she rewound the clips yet again.

Robyn turned her face away from the image of Tucker, beaten and swollen, hanging on the stage.

"I could leave that part out." Scarlet spoke quietly, her voice thick. A moment of silence passed, while the video scrolled without sound.

"We have to include it," Robyn said. "They need to understand."

Scarlet selected a few frames of Tucker and the MPs, but the majority were of the crowd. The film had captured a grainy, silent record of their rhythmic protest—

Silent.

Robyn's stomach knotted and she reached around Scarlet and pressed the Replay button.

"Hey," Scarlet complained. "I'm working here."

Security cameras recorded no sound. The people watching the video would have no idea what was going on.

"We blew it." Robyn's heart sank toward her toes. "No one is even going to hear the rain."

Scarlet grinned. "You underestimate me."

She punched a button on the console, and a little door popped open. A data card slid out, the kind that might've held photos on an old camera. When she popped it back in, the sound of the snapping, clapping crowd-effect rainstorm filled the room.

"You recorded sound?"

"Of course," Scarlet said. "What kind of amateur do you take me for?"

Robyn lay on her back on the server-room floor, listening to Scarlet pounding out keystrokes with the rhythm of a light rain. The room was silent other than the *tip tap tip tap tip tap* of her fingers.

"Is this even going to work?" Robyn asked.

"Everyone will see it," Scarlet promised. "The feed from the governor's mansion is not that well protected. We'll be able to use the same system Crown uses for his creepy announcements. Every TV in Sherwood will light up. But I don't want them to be able to trace the hack back to me."

"It'll air more than once?"

"As many times as we want."

$$\ggg\longrightarrow$$

It was like a freeze frame settled over the county. When the public loudspeakers hummed, and their private radios and televisions blurred with static, the people of Sherwood paused in fear. Mothers standing next to ironing boards, or bent over laundry baskets, held their breath. Plumbers squeezed up under sinks paused their wrenching against the pipes. Merchants froze in place

with their registers active, stuck in the act of scanning a customer's number. Here and there a vegetable-
slicing knife slipped, nicking a fingertip.

Shoppers in stores abandoned their baskets and
clustered toward any available screens, ready for the
inevitable. Pedestrians stopped on sidewalks to listen.
Only the smallest of their children ran in circles
around them and laughed, miraculously able to pretend
nothing was happening.

"Attention, Sherwood," came the voice through the
loudspeaker. An image rose on the screens, for those
who could see it.

The people braced themselves. *What new horrors will
Crown inflict now?* they wondered. It took a moment
for any of them to realize that the voice from the speaker
was different. It was not Crown's cool menace. It was
warm and light, the voice of a child. A girl.

"Attention all who care about the future of
Sherwood." The screen cut to a green arrow painted on
a brick wall. "We the people have something to say."

Images from the showcase began to play on the
screen. The boy being beaten before a crowd. The girl's
voice said, "Governor Crown and his Military Police
want to intimidate us with meaningless displays of
their power. Today, we showed them what our version
of power looks like."

The clip continued, as the workers responded with
their sounds of a storm.

"Remember that together we are many," the girl said. "Together we stand strong against tyranny."

The workers chanted, on and on, in a loop. The girl's voice echoed their cry. Soon, all across the county, whispered voices joined the chorus. "For Sherwood, unite. For Sherwood, we fight!"

≪CHAPTER THIRTY-THREE≫

Fragments and Followers

"This is unacceptable," Crown thundered. "She cannot get away with this."

"She's already gotten away with it, sir."

Crown glared at the underling who had brought him the news of Robyn's video hack. "You may go." The young man scurried out of the room, clearly relieved to be free of Crown's rage.

Crown turned to Bill Pillsbury, who was also in the room. "I mean there must be consequences. To stepping out of line in this manner."

"Naturally."

"I was being generous, allowing seventy-two hours for her to turn herself in. But the hoodlum has proven worthy of nothing less than the harshest judgment." He punched a button on his desk. "Get me Mallet," the governor barked into the intercom.

Shiffley strode into the room. "Hold that thought. You asked me to handle the hoodlum. You didn't want to call on Mallet anymore."

Crown acknowledged this by punching the button to disconnect the intercom. "We need a show of force."

"Such as?" Shiffley raised an eyebrow. Crown fought down a surge of frustration. If he said "show of force" to Mallet, she would know exactly what that meant. Damn it.

"It needs to happen every day now."

"We agreed it best if the showcases are less frequent," Pillsbury interjected "So they don't become inured to it."

Crown nodded. "At least for a while. Until they show that they can behave."

Shiffley lit up his PalmTab. "So, we should—"

"Take Loxley. Tonight."

"Robyn's deadline is tomorrow morning," Pill protested. "That would be going back on the timeline."

"The girl is not going to turn herself in," Crown mused. "Not as things stand right now. No more games. She'll know we're serious."

"I agree," Shiffley said.

"So do I," Pill acknowledged. "But I worry it looks like panicking. Not control."

Crown glared. "It looks like power."

"Very well," Pill said hesitantly.

"You aren't convinced?" Shiffley asked. "We should all be on the same page about this."

No, Crown thought. *You should all be on MY page.*

Pill shuffled, uncomfortable. "He's a friend. I suppose in the end, it's hard to forget that."

"I haven't forgotten," Crown replied.

"We were all on the same side once," Pill continued. "Do you ever think about that?"

"About what?" Crown snapped. "How many former friends turned against me?"

Pill held his instinctive response. Instead he said, "About how much the plan has changed since those days." He smiled. "Those dreamy lads might not recognize us."

"We were shortsighted back then." Crown laughed, a surprising small burst of joy that cut the tension in the room. "We have transcended what we once thought possible. Look at us now."

"Robyn will turn herself in, or she'll see her parents suffer," Shiffley said. "Right before her eyes. Ready the cameras for this one."

"Yes," Crown murmured. "She needs to see firsthand the pain that will come down upon her father if this nonsense does not end. She needs to feel *my* rain."

>>>→

Close to midnight, Robyn snuck out of the cathedral, bringing the green paint and the few scraps of moon lore cloth along with her. She retrieved them from their place on Tucker's book table, where they sat alongside the box and stick from Bridger. The, so far, *useless* box and stick.

Nessa would be broadcasting in a matter of minutes, once again calling on Sherwood to rise up and stand with Robyn. It was okay. She didn't need to hear the radio message personally. She skirted the checkpoint in the alley and climbed to the roof of a neighboring building, where she could lay out the curtain pieces and study them in the moonlight.

There were only snippets. One thing was immediately clear: these curtains had not been destroyed to be hidden and pieced together later. They had been sliced, torn, burned, shredded. They had not been meant to survive.

The only fragments that made sense said:

ARROW   HEART   FLAME   LIFE   SOUL

Robyn repeated the words to herself, turning them over and over in her mind. Fresh despair sliced through her as the clock in the square rang out midnight. Thirty hours until Crown's deadline. It wasn't enough time.

She tucked the scraps away and dashed across the rooftop to meet Scarlet. It was time to head toward the neighborhood they were assigned to tag.

"Sorry, I'm late," she whispered.

"No worries," Scarlet answered. They pulled out the first pair of green spray paint cans and descended to street level to get to work. "All right, so I'm going to do the row of shops east of Greenwood Street. You do west, and we'll meet at the corner of Iron Avenue?"

"That sounds right," Robyn agreed. "See you there in a few."

They headed off in opposite directions. As Robyn prepared to turn down the cross street, she paused. The smell of fresh spray paint reached her.

Something was off.

Next she heard the telltale ball bearing rattle and hiss.

Someone was painting in the wrong part of town.

They'd been really clear about which sections of town everyone would handle. Key had drawn simple maps, taking into account checkpoints and reasonable walking distances, and other logistics. He was good at that kind of thing.

"Scarlet," Robyn whisper-shouted, waving at her to come back. Had they come to the wrong neighborhood?

"Someone else is here?" Scarlet said, when she got closer.

"I guess. Let's find them." They ought to catch up with whoever it was so they could figure out who was in the wrong place. The girls turned the corner and followed the sound and smell of the paint.

"Over here," said a voice. "Let's do some on this wall."

"Okay, hurry," responded another person.

Something strange was happening. Robyn didn't recognize these voices.

She scurried ahead to the next intersection, but the taggers were already gone. Instead of chasing them, she stood and stared, with the mist of fresh paint still settling around her.

Scarlet came up behind her. "Whoa. Who did this?"

These arrows were not green. They were red and gold, and fancier than anything Robyn and her friends

had drawn the previous night. Also on the wall was another moon lore symbol: the circle and crescent that represented the sun and the moon. An echo of the pendant Robyn had lost to Sheriff Mallet.

Her hand automatically drifted to the place over her heart where it used to lie.

She and Scarlet walked around the next corner, ready to paint their own simple arrows. But there were already arrows and moon symbols everywhere. On the next street, too. And the next.

Scarlet looped an arm around Robyn's back. "So . . . does this mean we can get some sleep tonight?"

Robyn hugged her in return. "I think it means none of us will be sleeping much anytime soon!"

The strategy was working. Nessa's call had inspired the movement to grow.

≪CHAPTER THIRTY-FOUR≫

Behind the Wall

Robyn woke the next morning with the TexTer buzzing by her head.

CEASE ANTICS. C WILL SHORTEN D.

Forty-eight hours had already passed. How could he shorten the deadline now? If he did, wouldn't he announce it for everyone to hear?

Or, maybe not, if that would look too much like defeat. Robyn was in the process of proving she could do more harm in seventy-two hours than Crown could have predicted. She was getting the people of Sherwood ready to strike, beyond what she could manage herself. That had to bother him. Which was the whole point.

And what would be the point of shortening the deadline, without announcing it publicly? If Crown killed her parents before the deadline, Robyn would never turn herself in.

Now was the time to escalate antics, not cease them. Bill Pillsbury should know that. What if his TexTer had been compromised? She'd trusted him all of this time, but now she wasn't so sure.

Twenty-four hours remained. Robyn felt a little sick to her stomach. Once again she found herself second-guessing her choices. Perhaps they should be planning something bigger, something to really rattle Crown before the deadline.

They'd stolen guns, but wouldn't use them. They'd made a statement at the showcase. It had felt like a big deal at the time. Arrows appearing all over Sherwood was a statement unto itself.

Was it enough? How much difference did a little paint really make? The whole of Sherwood wasn't going to rise up within a day and march to the Castle District. It would take months, or more, to move people on that level. Why had it all seemed possible a few hours ago?

Had it ever really seemed possible? Not without the help of the moon lore, the pendant. Not without bringing all the Elements back together. Impossible things.

Robyn struggled again to put together the pieces she knew. She went up to the loft to look at Tucker's books. She couldn't look at them without thinking of what they had done to him at the showcase.

The books smelled musty and underused. She cracked them open again and tried to find something, anything that related to the words on the curtain fragments.

$$\ggg\!\!\longrightarrow$$

Mallet sat at her desk and fumed.

He hadn't called.

The hoodlum's piggybacked broadcast had aired all over Sherwood, every hour, on the hour, since dawn.

Still, Crown hadn't called. Apparently he was making good on his promise not to rely on Mallet anymore. That was a mistake, Ignomus. A big one.

Crown underestimated Mallet. He underestimated Robyn. Most of all, he underestimated the people of Sherwood. Their willingness to sacrifice, to fight teemed right below the surface of their obedience. Could he not see it?

If not, he was a fool. More so than Mallet had realized.

She would not make the same mistakes.

She resented the power the hoodlum held over the people of Sherwood: the power to dazzle, inspire, move them to action. In time, that power would become Mallet's own.

The techs in the basement were working overtime, tracking the location of the missing books. Each one, with its barcode, could be tracked within the library, the librarian had said. If each could be tracked within those walls, why not within the entire county?

She would find those books, and the knowledge they contained would help her on her journey. The clues within—the very clues Robyn herself was likely following—would give Mallet all she needed to predict the hoodlum's next moves and take back control.

Soon, it would be her time. Mallet could feel the power growing inside her. She fingered the black-and-white pendant on its chain.

Soon. And then, no one would be able to stand in her way.

>>⟶

Merryan found herself back in her uncle's suite again. Not for the first time today. Or the second. Seeing where he really lived made her feel like she could understand him better.

This time she stood in the bathroom and studied all the fixtures. The toilet and sink were a glossy white, the shower lined with gray stone tiles. The shower was quite large, really. Merryan stepped inside. It had a part in it that was L-shaped, a little indentation in the wall.

It had a low tile lip, grooved like an extra little soap dish, located about a quarter of the way up. She supposed for a lady, it would be the kind of place you could rest your foot while you shaved your legs.

She raised her foot onto the lip. Yes, it was about the right height for—whoa!

She wobbled and fell forward. She raised her arms to stop herself from falling into the wall, but the wall was moving.

She stumbled into a small closetlike room. Like the rest of the suite, the secret space was relatively spare. It was no treasure trove of secret objects, just one small trunk, barely bigger than a microwave. And a slender, high-backed armchair.

The trunk contained photographs. Dozens or hundreds.

Merryan had been wrong about her uncle. He wasn't completely cold. He was full of a sadness so intensely private, he literally hid it behind a wall and locked it away.

Walking out of the bathroom, Merryan froze. She found herself face-to-face with Crown. "Uh, Uncle Iggy," she stammered.

Her uncle took her by the arm and led her from the room.

"I'm sorry," she whispered as they walked quickly through the mansion halls. "I was just . . . I didn't know—"

"You want to know who I am." He spoke matter-of-factly, with overwhelming calm. "Come with me."

"Why?" Merryan whispered.

Crown flicked the question away with an arc of his eyebrow.

He led her down into the dungeon. Merryan refrained from explaining that she had been down there before. That she knew what they would find there. It was not likely to help her case.

But she was surprised.

The women were not seated on the earth floor as they had been the previous times Merryan had been down here. Now, they were chained to the wall. There were only two of them, wrists bound up above their heads, by wrist cuffs that looped through a chain on a hook. Their heads drooped. One was Mrs. Loxley. Merryan recognized the swirling crown of hair on her head, though she did not raise her head. On the arms and legs of both women, bruises erupted. They had been abused, manhandled. Interrogated.

"This is what happens to my enemies," Crown informed her. "This, or worse."

Merryan did not know what to say. "I thought they escaped," she said finally, averting her eyes. "I thought that's why you've been angry about my friends."

"Some escaped," said Crown. "Most. But we are tracking them down." He watched her closely for a moment, then he started to head back up the hallway. "Come along."

"You can't leave them there, like that," Merryan protested. "You have to let them down. They're not sup-posed to be chained."

"You misunderstand the way the world works," Crown responded. "I can do anything I want."

≪CHAPTER THIRTY-FIVE≫

Cracking the Code

Come afternoon, Robyn was still sitting among Tucker's books, trying to make sense of the puzzle pieces before her. She had Bridger's cloth scraps, Bridger's stick, a page on which she'd written the full curtain message.

She had found a few passages here and there that contained the curtain-scrap words:

"Soul of the people, speak with one voice"

"Like the tip of an arrow, hope spears the heart"

"Heart of the elements, flame renews life"

But just like the original curtain, these few cryptic sentences served only to confuse her further. The map had seemingly nothing more to give. The box wouldn't open. The stick—well, it was just a random stick, wasn't it? She picked it up.

It looked quite smooth, but it had some roughness on the edges. Robyn looked a little closer. The ends of the stick were not quite as sticklike as they first appeared. They were tapered, almost like a—Robyn gasped.

Like a key!

She grabbed the box, and stuck the end of the stick into the lock. It turned!

Bridger had given her the answer all along. *The arrow is the key* . . . Robyn opened the box. Hinged in the middle, it fell open easily to reveal two small items. One half held a stone arrowhead. The other half, a bundle of feathers. She pulled them out.

Suddenly it was obvious what to do. She took the stick and fixed the items to either end. This arrow symbolism was familiar. *Water, earth, air* . . .

Robyn's heart sped up. It was happening. She was finding the clues. Something was going to give. Somehow the answer would present itself. She held the arrow and stared at it, waiting. The answer was here. It had to be.

Footsteps on the creaky old stairs barely registered with her. A gruff voice behind her said, "It's looking downright scholarly in here."

Chazz eased up alongside Robyn and glanced at the books on the table. At the arrow in her hand.

"What does it mean?" she asked. The question wasn't only for him. It was for the air, the earth, the water, the elusive fire. A question for the Shadows and the Light.

"I guess it means you are the one," Chazz mused.

A burst of frustration surged through her chest. "But what does it *mean*?"

Chazz chuckled. "What do you think I know that you don't?"

Robyn shrugged. "You lied before." She whispered the truth out loud. "I'm not sure if I am the one, or if there even IS a 'one.'" She looked accusingly at Chazz. "You probably don't know, either."

He gazed back at her thoughtfully. "I guess none of us really know. It's a matter of faith."

Robyn shook her head. It wasn't enough. In the moment of silence that followed, she touched each clue again. Her hand glossed over the arrow Bridger had given her. The image in her mind now had nothing to do with the moon lore, but the fear in his face as the MPs had seized him.

The first time that happened Robyn had rushed forward to save him. Why hadn't she done that this time? Why had she run away like a scared child, only interested in her own well-being? She was supposed to be the one who could defeat the MPs. She was supposed to be the hero.

Chazz's hand followed hers. He picked up the arrow. "Everything we believe is fragile," he said. "They would have us believe it has all been destroyed. Or that it was never real to begin with." He held the slim wooden arrow shaft in his palm and extended it toward her. "Do you know what this is?"

Robyn shook her head. It had seemed small. Unimportant.

"The Arrow of Truth. One of many emblems that was allegedly destroyed."

"Emblems?" Robyn echoed.

Chazz shrugged. "The Arrow of Truth. The Pendant of Power. The . . . uh . . . there was a third thing, of course."

Robyn reached for the books again. She had the arrow. Mallet had the pendant. What could be the third thing? If she found it, could it help her?

"Look, here's what I do know," Chazz said. "Someone has to step up. And maybe it is written."

Robyn was already busy skimming pages. "Okay, maybe I'm blessed by the moon and everything about my story is preordained, but what if it isn't? What if there's more to figure out?"

"Does the story make you feel more powerful?" Chazz mused. "Believing it was written, that it's your destiny and calling—does that make it easier to step up?"

Robyn thought about this. "It makes it harder, I think. To know that everyone is looking at me."

Chazz's face lit up with sudden recognition. "The Cradle of Hope. That was the third strand."

"Strand? Like the braid?"

Chazz shook his head. "I don't have answers, girlie."

Robyn felt more words coming. She didn't want to say them to Chazz, but he was right there, and he seemed to be listening. "Where are the answers? Why can't I see them? All I see is the work laid out in front of me. Written or not, I could run from this place. I have a bike and some paper money and I could look for the edges of Nott City and just keep on driving. Like Dad said I should. Like *you* said I should."

"Why don't you?"

Honestly? "The thing inside me, the part of me that burns, it won't let me. I don't know if it's written. I don't know if it comes from the moon or the shadows, or if it's just the way of my own heart. But I can't let my parents down. I can't let the people down."

"Then I guess you have your answer."

"I started this hoodlum thing, and now their lives are on the line. Because of me. They can't have given up everything for me to do nothing."

Sacrifice. The word kept floating in and out of her mind. Sacrifice . . . like Laurel had done, and Tucker, and her mom. Like Bridger, too.

"I have to be worth it," she whispered. "Everyone is putting all their hopes in me. I have to become something better than myself, to be worth it."

Robyn stared at the books in desperation. In her heart of hearts, she knew there had to be more.

》》》⟶

Robyn ran her fingers through her shortened hair, wishing she could draw upon the strength of the absent braid.

She had found plenty of references to the "Arrow of Truth," the "Pendant of Power," the "Cradle of Hope," and so on. The curtain words were turning out to be somewhat common in the mix, but she didn't find them coming together in any way that felt like a message to her.

It was looking bleak.

The one who will come as the Fire brings new light to the people in shadow.

Sure.

An arrow pierces the heart as surely as the light pierces the shadows.

Okay.

The flame that can flow as blood creates life even in the lee of the strongest boulder.

Whatever.

Tucked in between pages of one of the books, she found a sheet of paper with Tucker's handwriting. An excerpt from his dissertation? A quote from another book? The notations were unclear, but the message was legible:

You're clinging to things of the distant past. Put your eye to the future instead.

Further down, it read:

The shrines have burned. You want to have faith because your father has faith. But the world is not black and white.

*The answers aren't written in curtains or texts. It's you,
in the world, who finds the answers.*

Robyn slammed the book shut on the paper. This
was no help.

She had only twenty-four hours. It was a matter of
life and death, which felt pretty black and white to her.
If mystical energies were going to converge upon her, and
transform her into some kind of hero, they had better
do it soon.

The braid shop was a dead end. And it was still dangerous to try to get back to the tree house. Too many
guards, too much risk. But . . . it might be the only
chance she had left.

≪CHAPTER THIRTY-SIX≫

Unintended Consequences

"Nottingham Cathedral?" Mallet listened as the lab tech explained his work to locate the library books.

"Well, that's as close as we can estimate, yeah. They must be somewhere within a block of there, one direction or another. The barcodes are not designed to work outside the library walls. The farther the distance from the system itself, the broader the location results are bound to be."

"Good enough," Mallet said. "I'll head over there now."

Nottingham Cathedral had been boarded up for some years now. From the looks of the place, it was likely condemned. Mallet circled the block, studying the neighboring buildings. None looked like a desirable place to study. She had been expecting apartment buildings, a row of houses, a coffee shop or restaurant. Any place a college student might frequent. But instead, everything here was commercial and industrial. With a great deal boarded up, to boot.

The older man appeared as if from nowhere. One moment the block was empty. The next, there he was, hunched and hurrying, his shoulders tucked forward as if he was warding off rainfall.

"Ma'am," he said, tapping his forehead as if to tip his hat to her. Mallet nodded, then turned to watch him as he passed. His hand stayed raised, along the side of his face, as if to conceal his scruff of beard, or the scar along his jaw, or the strange crook of his broad nose. He circled around a corner, and she began to follow after him. Instinct.

Something was up here.

Where had he come from? Why did he look so familiar?

Mallet tapped her PalmTab. "Get me a secure perimeter around Nottingham Cathedral."

$$\ggg\!\!\longrightarrow$$

Tucker's sweaty fingers slipped from the wheelbarrow handle. The barrow listed to the side, spilling half of its contents back onto the ground. *Great.* As he bent to scoop up the spilled gravel, his body complained about the motions. He was still wounded and sore all over.

The sound of bursting voices erupted behind him. Tucker immediately regretted the impulse to turn and look. A trio of guards thumped across the gravel toward him. One had an arm outstretched, pointing in Tucker's direction.

"Oh no. Oh boy." Tucker started to panic. They had seen him slip. They were coming to punish him.

"It's okay," Robert said from alongside him. "One spill is not a big deal." He leaned on his shovel handle and studied the men approaching them. He added, "This is about something else."

The guards stormed up to them. "Loxley?"

Robert nodded shortly.

"Come with us." The guards grasped him by the arms. "Looks like it's your turn to take the stage."

Everyone paused their work as Robert was taken away from the gravel camp. When he was gone, the other men clustered closer to Tucker with their shovels. Helping him clean up his wheelbarrow spill was a good excuse to get close enough to talk.

"What did they say?"

"Not much." Tucker repeated the exchange. He righted the wheelbarrow and held it while the others worked to fill it back up. The cuts and bruises on his back made it painful to move his muscles. But he had no choice.

"Another showcase?" one of the men muttered. "Already?"

"You said it would be once every week," Tucker said. "Why is it happening the next day?"

No one knew the answer, but everyone grew agitated, wondering.

≪CHAPTER THIRTY-SEVEN≫

Warnings

Key leaned back in the creaky desk chair and propped his feet on the corner of the desk. He stared at the chipped plaster ceiling. His thinking pose.

Currently, he was thinking about drawers. All the lonely compartments within a single block of wood. All the things they contained.

He knew without looking that the drawers in this desk had brass handles. Except for the one that was missing a handle, the one they could never get open. He wondered what was in it. Wondering what was in it made him think about secrets. And mysteries. All the drawers of the world he could not figure out how to open.

The problem with being a thinker and a planner was that you always needed to know all the facts in order to think things through and make a good plan. He liked arithmetic and long division, not algebra.

Real life was too much like algebra. There was always an unknown.

Robyn was like a person-version of algebra, Key thought. Always a puzzle to everyone else, and always thinking she was solving something.

She had no idea the length of the struggle that had preceded her. No sense of the history. She thought of the moment things changed for *her* as the beginning of everything. Her life had been perfect, up until a few months ago. Robyn didn't talk so much about her home, but Laurel had described it. The large white house with too many rooms to count. The wide sweeping lawn. The cameras. It all told a story.

Key tried not to be jealous of Robyn's easy Castle District life. He reminded himself how much worse his life might have been if he had been raised there like she was. There was no use imagining. He felt guilty for even thinking about it. He had been raised in a poor but loving family, although they were gone now, and he didn't much want to think about that, either.

The drawers in this desk had smoothed edges after years of finger touching. They had probably been opened hundreds of times. They tended to stick. You had to give them a good tug.

He tugged slightly on the drawer handle. Listened to the sound of sliding, rolling. The sound alone was satisfying.

He tugged a little harder. Sliding. Rolling.

He pushed the drawer back in.

$$\ggg\!\!\longrightarrow$$

Merryan lay in her bed, teasing the mound of crumpled tissues beside her. The guard was back outside her door. Her uncle was as much of a monster as everyone said. Mrs. Loxley and the other woman were suffering just a few floors below her feet and there was nothing she could do. Robyn was surely in danger, somewhere, with whatever her uncle was planning. Everything was terrible, and only getting worse.

A knock came at the door.

"Go away," Merryan said.

The guard spoke through the door. "Miss Crown, the governor would like to see you in his office."

It was early evening. Not late enough to claim to be sleepy. But Merryan considered refusing the call, anyway. He couldn't just summon her every time he wanted to say something. Couldn't he walk up the stairs to her room, like a normal guardian? But that wasn't what monsters did, apparently.

She trudged dutifully down to his office, wishing her rebel streak was stronger. Wishing his horribleness made her care less about him. Wishing he could become the kind of person she, and the whole city, deserved.

"Something you said has stuck with me," he told her. "The idea that I accompany you to Sherwood."

A blip of hope crossed Merryan's radar. "If you could see what I do there, maybe you'd understand. Maybe you'd want to help, too."

Crown's smile was cold. "I am who I am, you know."

"I just thought—"

"My wife tried to change me. My colleagues tried. There is no use in these games. I am a man who will have his way at any cost."

Merryan could see that to be true. It was hurtful, and scary, and sad.

"If you are going to live within these walls, it is only fair that you come to know me."

"You've said that already." Merryan sniffled.

"No school tomorrow. You wanted me to come to Sherwood with you. Wishes come true, my dear girl. You'll be right beside me when I take this hoodlum down."

He spoke of Robyn in a different kind of tone than he had previously. Perhaps he had realized where Merryan's true loyalties lay. So she didn't bother to hide her dismay at the thought.

Her uncle smiled. "The whole world will suffer as I have suffered. And I will never apologize."

Merryan spun on her heel and swept out of his office. She had to find a way to warn Robyn!

Merryan hurried down the hallway, and burst into Bill Pillsbury's office.

"I'm interested in communications," she said.

Pill raised his eyebrows. "Oh?"

"Yes," she said hurriedly. She didn't know how much time she had before the guards might come looking for her. "I want to learn how to talk to people better."

"PR training?" Pill mused. This was a turn. He had, of course, seen her in the hallway with Robyn and the other children. Helping the women from the dungeon escape. He had gained more respect for Merryan after that, but he couldn't risk her blowing his cover.

"May I speak freely?" Merryan asked.

"I wouldn't recommend it in this space." Pill twirled a finger as if to indicate cameras or bugs in the ceiling. The castle was wired, Merryan knew, but she couldn't imagine anyone was actually listening to every room at once.

"Communications, PR, it's not about speaking freely," Pill explained. "It's about saying exactly what needs to be said to the listening parties. No wasted words. No mistakes."

"Yes," Merryan said. "I tend to blurt. And babble."

Pill knew this to be true. The poor girl was constantly flustered.

"If I have a message, can you help me craft it?"

"Interesting. What sort of message did you have in mind?" He hoped the girl was capable of choosing her words carefully.

Merryan nodded. "Well, there's nothing I have to say that—" she paused. "I mean, Uncle Iggy already knows how I feel."

"I was wondering," he said. "I heard your rather heated discussion yesterday."

"The kids who broke into the mansion. They—I thought they were my friends. And I can't get back," she said, looking Pill in the eye. "I can't get back at them. There's so much I want to say, but I can't let anyone know how I feel. Uncle Iggy says never let anyone see when you're hurt."

"I can imagine his perspective on that," Pill kept his tone noncommittal.

"I thought since you are a communications expert, you could help me figure out what to say."

"What do you want to say?"

Merryan's eyes flashed. "Don't underestimate me. I have my uncle's ear, and he's coming for you."

"I imagine they already know," Pill replied amiably.

"They won't come back here. They can't. So I'm sending him to them. I need them to know what is coming. Can you help me?"

"I believe I can, yes." Pill smiled thoughtfully as the governor's niece slipped out of his office. The last thing Merryan Crown needed was communications training.

◄CHAPTER THIRTY-EIGHT►

Perimeter Peril

Robyn strode into the office. Key was sitting at the desk looking pensive. He jumped about a mile when she walked in.

"What?" she said. "You didn't hear me coming?"

"It's cool." Key smiled, fumbling with something in his pocket. "I guess I was just too far into my own head."

"I need to go out for a little while," Robyn said. "I'll be back well before midnight. I want to be here to hear what happens when Nessa goes on."

"You like my idea?" Key asked hesitantly. "About the broadcast tonight?"

"Yeah, I think it's great," Robyn answered. "It fits our pattern. The arrows were everywhere, the rainstorm was everyone. This will be everywhere *and* everyone. I'm—"

"Robyn!" Scarlet shouted from within the server room. "Robyn, get in here!"

Robyn and Key scrambled down the hall to join Scarlet there. It was six p.m. Twelve hours before Crown's deadline. Twelve hours before anyone had expected anything more to happen.

"There's another showcase going on," Scarlet announced. "Look!" She pointed to the monitors which carried the live footage of the showcase square.

"They've escalated?" Key sounded surprised. "We must have really freaked them out yesterday."

"I'm not prepared for this," Scarlet complained. "We could be up there filming. If they do the rain again, it would be powerful to have a second day's footage."

"They won't do the rain," Key guessed. "Look at the MPs around the square. They've more than doubled their force."

Meanwhile, the cameras scrolled through the live footage of the square, and the stage, and the face of the man in the chains. Robyn stared, speechless, at the screen.

"What is it?" Key asked, tapping her arm.

"That's . . ." Robyn's throat closed on her. "That's my dad."

She couldn't tear her eyes from the screen that showed her father. Her heart dipped and soared between relief that he was really alive and despair over what would happen to him. Up until now it had been an idea in her head.

Jeb rushed in. "The MPs have been ordered to set up a perimeter around this cathedral. We have to get out. Now!"

Scarlet jumped to her feet. Key and Robyn spun around, ready to run.

In the past few months, the friends had talked at length about escape procedures if the cathedral was breached. They kept rope ladders in the bell towers. They'd cracked the seal on a couple extra windows. There was a cupboard in the basement that could fit three people, and several dozen spots that a single person could hide.

There was no contingency plan for an MP perimeter.

"How much time do we have?" Scarlet asked.

"Half an hour. Maybe less," Jeb said. "I happened to be already arriving. We got lucky."

"A perimeter. What does that really mean?" Robyn asked. "Closer checkpoints? They're not coming inside?"

"I don't think anyone knows it's possible to get inside," Jeb said. "But we can't be sure. And we can't be seen coming or going. This place is no longer safe."

Scarlet was already shutting down her systems and unplugging things left and right. Jeb began helping her pack up as much of the equipment as possible. "We don't have time for this," he insisted.

"It'll take ages to replace it all. I need this stuff. I'm not leaving without it."

Key ran to the office to pack up the remaining paint.

Robyn dashed to the choir loft. She gathered the moon lore items still scattered on the desk.

They fled the cathedral, just in time to avoid the perimeter MPs arriving. The line of jeeps converged on the cathedral area and the friends split up, carrying their separate loads in several directions.

"Catch you on the flip side," Scarlet called as they parted.

"See you soon," Robyn said, tossing her a wave. For once, their running in opposite directions felt like solidarity.

The planned rendezvous would be much later, at the fire. For now, they deliberately planned not to lead any pursuers back toward T.C. No doubt that would be the first place Mallet's MPs would think to look. But now Robyn found herself drifting in that direction, anyway. She hefted the satchel over her shoulder and hurried along.

It was now or never, Robyn realized. She'd put off venturing back to the tree house because the Crescendo seemed to need her constant attention. But now, alone and on the run, it was the only obvious place to go.

When she'd left there last, she'd been upset. She'd stumbled down the stairs, and seen something on the bottom of the tree house. The only remaining hope was to look there. It would be risky to go into the woods at night. She'd have to get past the patrolling guards. But she had no choice. There was too much at stake.

Seeing her dad chained up onstage, surrounded by MPs, made Crown's threat seem all too real. How had she imagined she would be able to waltz in and save him at the last minute? All this time, her mind was playing tricks on her.

If there were answers in the moon shrines, she needed them now.

Only one curtain was whole, and it was out of reach behind the locked door. Everything else was in fragments.

She was only one girl.

And she had just been run out of the closest thing she had to a home. The protection of the cathedral had bolstered her confidence. Now she felt exposed.

Crown was gunning for her, big-time. How was she ever going to fix it all? How was she going to save them?

⋘CHAPTER THIRTY-NINE⋙

Reunited

Robyn ran into the woods, trying to convince herself that all was not lost. She had no home now, on either side of the woods. Her parents were about to be killed, and she did not have a full plan for how to save them. No matter how many times she told herself she might have to let them go to serve the Crescendo, now that push was coming to shove, she knew she couldn't let it happen. She had less than twelve hours to come up with a REAL plan, not one based on hope and smoke and mirrors.

She climbed the tree house steps, trying to get close enough to study the base of the structure. It was hard to see through the leaves and vines. She returned to the trunk and looked upward. There was something there, but she'd have to get closer. She held the scraps of fabric in the slices of moonlight that filtered through the leaves.

ARROW   HEART   FLAME   LIFE   SOUL

Nothing had changed about the scraps, or their words. The curtain messages reiterated the teamwork element. That was the part she already knew. But what about the part that was hers alone? The part where she became the fire and knew how to save everyone.

She moved the fragments around, trying to find an order that sparked some recognition, some answers.

A prickle rose on the back of her neck. Robyn sensed she wasn't alone.

Leaves rustled, too close to the ground to be caused by wind, and the soft sound of labored breathing approached. Robyn spun toward the sound, ready to fight.

Out of the darkness, Laurel launched herself at Robyn, smothering the older girl in the sort of hug a giant starfish might give.

"By the moon," Robyn cried out. "Laurel!"

The girls fell to the ground, limbs all twisted together. They laughed as they landed in a pile of sticks and leaves. Laurel clung to Robyn so tightly, she started to feel like a balloon about to pop.

"It's good to see you, too," Robyn managed to eke out. "But it would be even better if I could breathe."

"Oops," Laurel said, untangling herself from her friend. "I'm just so happy."

They sat up.

"Oh, I'm so glad you're all right!" Robyn brushed leaves out of Laurel's matted hair. "You're alive. How did you get away?"

"They took us to a room, and then I ran." She blurted out the story in a rapid breathless burst.

Robyn's eyes clouded over. "My mom?"

Laurel shook her head. "I don't know much. I just ran for it."

Robyn pushed down the tiny surge of anger that rose inside her. It wasn't fair to be upset. Laurel couldn't be expected to save Mrs. Loxley all on her own. It was a miracle she'd managed to get herself out. Like Laurel always said, you could get out of anywhere if you're small.

Robyn hugged her friend again.

"You had to leave them," Robyn reassured her. "You'd still be a prisoner, too, if you hadn't." She hugged the smaller girl once again.

"I wish it was different," Laurel whispered.

"Now," Robyn said. "Look what I found."

Robyn and Laurel studied the moon lore scraps. Laurel shimmied up the tree trunk to get a closer look at the underside of the tree house. "It was a curtain," she reported. "But all the fabric has been sawed off."

"Sawed?" Robyn said. That was an odd choice of words.

Laurel skidded back down. "Well, sawed, or chewed or something. Rough cuts."

"The shrines were truly destroyed." Robyn sighed, resigned to this not-knowing. "The messages weren't meant to survive."

Laurel leaned against Robyn's shoulder and sighed. "I'm sleepy. Can we go home now?"

Robyn's heart twisted. Laurel didn't know the truth yet. "You can spend the night in the tree house, if you want. The cathedral's not safe."

"What?" Laurel looked alarmed. "My paintbrush sheets?"

Robyn laughed. Of course that was what she'd be worried about. Not the loss of life and limb, but the loss of her favorite sheets. "We'll see," she said. "Either we'll get back into the cathedral, or we'll get you a new set of sheets."

"Is everyone safe?"

"I don't know," Robyn admitted. "We all kind of ran for it. And then I came here. I have to go back."

"Why wouldn't they all come to the tree house? Where else would everyone go?"

"Evacuation plan. They all scattered," Robyn mused. "I have to go meet them, but you can sleep here."

"No, I want to stay with you."

"Then we should go. They'll be waiting."

>>>⟶

When Laurel and Robyn got to Tent City, the others were hunkered around the fire, clearly waiting for them. Robyn stepped into the firelight first.

"Where have you been?" Key seemed annoyed. "You had us worried."

"I was coming," Robyn said. "I got delayed. And look what I found in the woods."

She turned and held up her hands like a game-show model revealing the grand prize. Laurel strolled out of the shadows, grinning from ear to ear.

"Hey!" The group cheered in welcome.

Scarlet leaped up and hugged Laurel.

"Everyone's okay?" Robyn asked.

"Yeah," Scarlet said. "Thanks to Jeb's warning."

"We're talking about our plans."

"My parents?" Robyn asked. "Is there any news?" There hadn't been time to assess the situation fully while fleeing the cathedral.

Key broke the news gently. "They've still got your dad in chains on the showcase stage. They plan to leave him there all night."

Scarlet pulled up the feed on her tablet. The images were grainy, pirated from nighttime security footage. Robert Loxley stood alone on the stage. The sight of him tugged her heart. It would be a long night for him, unable to sit or relax.

"With no guards?" Robyn's mind lit up with the possibilities of rescue.

Scarlet scanned the area cameras for any sign of movement in the square. "Crown's daring you to come tonight."

The fantasy fizzled. "Then it's probably a trap."

Key agreed. "We could double bluff him and go, anyway."

The crackle of logs filled the moment of silence.

"*Hmm*. They brought Dad to the public stage. Why?" Robyn tapped her chin. "Mallet probably hopes to catch me quietly tonight and then lord it over Sherwood tomorrow, by having us both in chains."

"Not on our watch," Laurel piped in.

"Exactly," Robyn agreed. "We need a plan. As public as possible."

She leaned toward the fire. She breathed in the heat.

"Come dawn, we show Crown what the people of Sherwood are made of."

≺CHAPTER FORTY≻

The Secret of the Sphere

Mallet fumed as she listened to reports by her junior MPs regarding the transfer of Robert Loxley. The orders had come down through channels, they reported. They seemed surprised that she wasn't pleased with their work.

"You've got him on the showcase stage? Right now?"

"That's affirmative. Do you want us to take him back?" the young MP asked nervously.

"No. You did fine." Mallet held her anger. Better to release it upon those who truly deserved it. "But do keep checking in with me." She ended the call.

Orders like that should come down from her office alone. But no. Shiffley was jumping the gun. She'd have to—

A knock came at her office door.

"Yeah?" Mallet barked.

Her head lab tech entered the office. "I've found something you might want to take a look at."

"The library books?" Mallet asked.

"Actually no. An older project, from a few months ago."

"I don't have time for that now."

The tech strode forward, anyway. He placed a small silver sphere on Mallet's desk. "Remember this?" he asked.

Mallet picked up the metallic sphere. She studied the inscription: *Breath, Blood, Bone.*

"It was confiscated, the day we burned the tents," Mallet said. The day Robyn Hoodlum became more than just a nuisance but a leader and a threat.

"Robyn recorded her own message over it, as you'll recall."

Mallet nodded. "I remember."

"The sphere was significantly damaged, though," the tech said. "So it's unclear if Robyn, or anyone, ever saw the original message in its entirety."

"But you can play it now?"

"Yes." The lab tech played the hologram. Robert Loxley's face and form appeared. The sphere projected him into the room in front of them.

"Robyn, honey, if you're receiving this message, I fear the worst has happened. Listen closely, love, for there is much I will need you to do now.

"I'm sorry you will be alone to deal with the challenges ahead. There are many others who can help you, but you will have to also find strength within.

"You must visit the shrines. Gather the elements. They will be your closest friends. But you have a special role to play. The moon lore has promised us there is one who can save us. One who will lead us through darkness and light, and Robyn, the signs suggest you could be the fire our people are waiting for.

"You have to choose to trust the moon. These words are for you and you alone: a gift passed down through our family. The ancient map of Sherwood holds many secrets: the path to the shrines, the truth in every arrow. Your pendant is the key. My half plus Mom's will open the door.

"You must conceal your Tag to stay off the radar. Wear the gloves everywhere you go. Like the fire, you are strong and brave. I love you and I believe in you always."

One thing was very clear after watching the hologram Robert Loxley had created for his daughter: the love and devotion they felt for each other. He'd gone as far as to gift the child with the Pendant of Power.

Mallet lifted the charm and studied it. Black stone, in a cool curving arc, nestled around the white oval that gradually warmed against her palm.

The message about the shrines rang true. The legend of the one who could be as the fire. Mallet remembered these lessons from when she was very small. The chosen one would bear the pendant, the key to great power.

Mallet stroked the pendant. Its power was hers now. The hoodlum was all that stood in her way.

Robyn was not likely to turn herself in as a result of Crown's ultimatum. But the girl would be equally unwilling or unable to stand by and watch her loving parents destroyed. Shiffley thought he was rubbing his victory in the hoodlum's face? No, actually, his premature actions had given Robyn and her friends plenty of notice as to how, when, and where the Loxleys would be dealt with.

Yes, Mallet was sure that Robyn would be there in the morning, ready to wreak havoc. The city was already teeming with graffiti symbols, indicating that Robyn's rebellion had a stronger foothold than anyone had realized.

There would be consequences to standing against Crown. There would be more consequences for standing against Mallet. She called in her senior MPs to begin planning for the morning showcase.

No way she'd let Nick Shiffley waltz up onto that stage and take credit for ridding Sherwood of Robyn Hoodlum.

⊰CHAPTER FORTY-ONE⊱

All the Possible

They were sitting around the fire, close to achieving a plan, when the TexTer buzzed. "It's Pillsbury," Robyn said.

C COMING TO YOU. 6AM

The friends looked at each other in surprise. "Does that mean what I think it means?" Scarlet said. "I mean, is there some other way to interpret it?"

"No," Robyn said slowly. "Crown is coming to the showcase." She looked at the sky. "Of course he's coming. He wants to be there when I turn myself in."

Scarlet agreed. "Or in case you don't. To still show everyone who's really in charge."

Key jumped to his feet. "This is amazing. We'll get him. Tomorrow." He paced in place, and murmured, "Crown will die tomorrow."

"Uh, what?" Scarlet said. "That's a little dramatic."

Nessa Croft looked skeptical. "Crown leaving Castle District means a lot of extra security. We need to rethink everything."

"The basic plan will still work," Scarlet argued. "We resist. And we record it all. Whether he's there or not."

Key groaned in annoyance. "Crown is coming to us. We never expected that! We can't let this opportunity pass us by."

"We won't," Robyn said.

"But it doesn't mean killing him," Nessa said. "Obviously we can't do that."

It wasn't obvious to Key. "Crown has to die. That's how this ends. Why can't you all see it?"

Robyn watched him stirring the air with his fists. Strange. Key's anger was normally a slow steady simmer. All under the surface, with small bubbles occasionally ranging to the top. Now, it was boiling over. He seemed eager to scald the whole world.

If anyone should be full of rage at Crown it was her. And yet, knowing he'd be there tomorrow gave her a surprising feeling of calm. "No one is going to die tomorrow," she vowed. "Especially not my parents."

Key looked at her. "Crown's mistake was not killing all the Parliament. When we free them, their work can continue. We don't want to make the same mistake with Crown."

The coldness of his words gave Robyn a chill. "Those are my parents you're talking about. Not killing them was a mistake? Whose side are you on?"

"You know what I mean. You know I'm right."

"What happened?" Robyn asked. "Why do you always want us to fight that way?"

"We're not killers," Scarlet said softly. "We can talk about it and think about it, but it's not even real."

"We have no weapons," Laurel said. "We don't want any."

The other three exchanged glances. It was impossible to forget the storeroom full of guns at their disposal. But that wasn't the way to beat Crown. And they all knew it. Even Key, Robyn was sure.

"We stick with the original plan," Robyn said. "Tomorrow's about stopping the MPs, and rescuing my parents. If Crown will be there, fine. If we can get him, too, all the better."

"Right," said Laurel and Scarlet.

Key said nothing.

$$\gg\!\!\longrightarrow$$

Nessa left the group at the fire well before midnight, so that she could to find a place to broadcast. Thousands of old radios tuned to the chosen frequency. Thousands of ears bent toward the speakers to listen.

"*Crown may put up his walls and checkpoints; we will not go quietly. He may hoard our food and try to enslave us; we will not starve to do his work. We will fight.*"

The people listened with a mix of excitement and fear.

"*Robyn won't let you down. Don't you let her down, either. We are in this together.*"

Some of the people listening were workers who had been part of the rain demonstration at the showcase. Others had fingertips stained from paint. Some felt too fearful to try, but still hopeful.

"*The storm has come. Crown is feeling our rain. All over Sherwood, he can see the signs of rebellion.*"

The people had seen the signs, too. They knew it was true.

"*The Crescendo is in our blood. The storm is all of us.*"

Nessa then invited people to open their windows. "*Sing with me. Sing out into the streets. Let them know that we won't be silenced.*"

She began singing.

"*Gather the Elements as you will: Earth to ground you, Water to fill. Air to sustain, a Fire to ignite; Elements gather, all to fight.*"

The voices rang through the streets. They came from within houses, they came from passersby. There were MPs in the ranks who recognized the tune, though they dared not sing along.

"*Gather the Elements as you will: till Earth cannot shake us, nor Water be still; Air, boundless, our everything; the Fire, our true light; Elements gather, all to fight.*"

The music was everywhere. Soon, the sound reached the group of young rebels sitting in a circle around the Tent City fire. They gazed at each other in wonder.

》》→

It was approaching midnight when Sheriff Mallet left her office. She walked through the courtyard of the Sherwood Central Office Building Complex and got into her personal vehicle. The driver was ready and waiting.

"Good evening, Sheriff."

She nodded to him, but she was lost in thought. The singing from the hologram haunted her. As the car pulled away from the curb, she could almost still hear it. The same song. Very faint, but very clearly . . . She had to snap out of it.

But as the car carried her through the neighborhoods toward home, the song became more insistent. It wasn't in her head.

"Stop the car," she ordered her driver. The vehicle slowed. Mallet rolled down her window.

The singing had no clear source, and yet it filled the air. Her PalmTab lit up with reports from MPs across the city. Nessa Croft was singing on the radio. The people of Sherwood had opened their windows to join her.

It was the kind of subversive act that had power. No arrests could be reasonably made. Not enough arrests, anyway. And not in time.

A few citizens gone missing here or there would not be enough to scare the entire population into silence.

Crown had seriously misjudged his opponent. Mallet wouldn't make the same mistake. Tomorrow, she'd be ready.

⫷CHAPTER FORTY-TWO⫸

According to Plan

The governor's motorcade arrived about the time that the workers started filing into the square. For many, it was unusual and unexpected to be corralled into the showcase square in the morning time. For most, though, it was a slow march fraught with nervous anticipation.

Sheriff Mallet was already there, with her full crew of MPs. She was surprised to see Crown's entire motorcade pulling up. She had been expecting Shiffley, and a handful of guards.

Crown's presence changed everything.

The stage was set up much as it had been the day before. The main difference: there was a third wooden pole and two sets of chains. Robert Loxley already stood chained in one half, where he had remained throughout the night. Seemingly unguarded.

Robyn had not taken the bait. Shiffley had no doubt been expecting the girl to stage some kind of middle-of-the-night rescue attempt. Surely he'd had guards hidden around the square, waiting to close in.

Mallet shook her head. Yes, Robyn's hoodlum acts mostly took place sneakily and at night. But Robyn was too smart to fall for someone else's shadowy tricks. She was trying to start a movement. Today, she needed an audience.

And Shiffley was making sure she had one. Fool.

Mallet pulled back her shoulders and adjusted her sidearm. This showcase was bound to get interesting.

$$\ggg\!\!\longrightarrow$$

Crown's guards brought Mrs. Loxley out of one of the motorcade cars and led her up onto the stage. They chained her up alongside her husband.

Crown got out of his car and Merryan started to follow him, but he closed the door between them.

"Lock her in," Crown ordered. The driver tapped his PalmTab and the doors latched with a *crunch*.

Merryan's eyes widened. She tugged the door handle, but was helplessly trapped. "Uncle Iggy?"

"You can see everything just fine from there," her uncle told her through the glass.

He climbed the stairs to the wooden stage as the square continued to fill with Sherwood workers.

"Marissa." He nodded to the sheriff, who eyed him with a peculiar combination of annoyance and admiration.

"Ignomus," she responded.

His eyes flashed at her impudent tone. She should know by now not to provoke him. And yet the more she stood up to him, the harder it was to look away.

"What are you doing here?" she asked him, not loud enough for the crowd to hear. She could challenge him all she wanted, one-on-one, but the unified front was important to their shared power.

"I'm here to kill Robert Loxley," he said. "And to take Robyn Hoodlum into custody."

Mallet shook her head. In her gut she wanted to argue. This was not the way to take the girl down. "What makes you think she'll really show?" she asked instead.

Crown looked out over the square. "She'll show." He clipped his portable microphone to his collar. Before tapping it on, he added, "That little hoodlum loves an audience. She won't be able to help herself."

With that Crown stepped forward and began to address the gathering crowd, his voice projected over the square. "This special showcase has been brought to you by your so-called friend and standard bearer, Robyn Hoodlum."

"Robyn is our hero," Mrs. Loxley said, from her place in the stockade. Her voice was weak. Her body sagged against the chains. "Robyn, we love you."

Crown folded his hands behind him and waited for the murmurs across the square to settle. He pointed back at Mr. and Mrs. Loxley. "These rebels have been a thorn in my side for too long. Their daughter, your would-be hero, doesn't care about them."

"You'll never win, Ignomus," Robert Loxley shouted. "Sherwood forever!"

Crown whipped around and smacked him hard across the face. Then with a wave of his hand, he ordered the couple gagged. MPs dashed up onstage and stuffed cloth into the prisoners' mouths.

The crowd surged with muttered words of outrage, and the occasional echo of "Sherwood forever!" rose up like popcorn from a few people spread across the sea of workers.

"I'm a reasonable man," Crown said. "I've given the hoodlum a chance to save these rebels, and she has declined. What kind of hero leaves her family to suffer?"

Crown was on a roll. "If she won't stand up to save them, what makes any of you think she cares and will stand up for you?" He pounded his fist against the air. "I am the one who cares about Sherwood. I am the one who will make Nott City great again!"

Sheriff Mallet tried to keep from laughing out loud. *Robyn* loved an audience? That was the pot calling the kettle black. Crown was the only one grandstanding here. If anything, he was giving Robyn a platform to make even more of a name for herself.

Mallet could see the next hour unfolding like clock-work. Robyn would refuse to appear. Crown would be forced to kill her parents in front of hundreds. Robyn would emerge as the sympathetic, sacrificial orphan, and the whole of Sherwood would rise up to support her.

The question was, could Mallet turn the tide of Robyn's rebellion to her own favor?

≫⟶

Robyn, Scarlet, Key, and Laurel stood on the nearby rooftop watching the showcase gearing up. Crown's opening speech speared them with rage.

"Everyone understands how to use the earpieces?" Scarlet confirmed.

The four friends all touched their ears in unison.

"Yeah," Laurel said. "This is cool."

Jeb had given them small listening devices that allowed them to communicate while on the move. The small rubber earbud poked into the ear canal and was held in place by a plastic hook over the rim of the ear. All they had to do was touch the outer rim to talk to each other. It had taken several weeks for Jeb to sneak enough of the devices out of the MP stores. And it had taken Scarlet even longer to hack them to change the frequencies to match each other, but not the MPs'. This would be their first time using the earpieces, and it couldn't have come at a better moment.

"It's about half an hour to the deadline," Key said. "Time to take our positions."

≫⟶

Robyn secured her beret atop her head and tucked the sewn-in braid over her shoulder. In one hand, she clutched the Arrow of Truth. For courage. As she moved through the crowd, people recognized her. The workers parted for her, then closed ranks behind her. Their whispered encouragement bolstered her confidence.

"We knew you'd come."

"Thanks for what you're doing."

"We're behind you."

"We believe in you!"

"We won't let them get to you."

Folded into the sea of large men, she felt protected and emboldened. It was time to go to work.

Up onstage, Crown was still speaking. He spewed the same tired slogans over and over. He taunted. He dared Robyn to show her face, dared her to show up and challenge him. He seemed almost delirious, high on his own power. He was ready to close in for the kill.

Robyn didn't have a fancy lapel microphone. But she did have a way to project her voice. She raised the digital megaphone to her lips and began to shout.

"You wanted me here, Crown? You've got me," she said. "But you will never take me down."

The device was only the size of her fist, but it made her voice enormous. Robyn's words echoed up from within the heart of the crowd.

"No one is going to die today," Robyn announced. Her words had been carefully scripted, according to the plan. "Not on my watch."

From another spot in the square, Laurel waited patiently for her cue to send up the signal. She was nervous. She felt small. But she was following the plan.

Up on the rooftop, Scarlet pounded away at her keyboards. "Just another couple seconds," she muttered to herself. She was nervous. She felt slow. But she was following the plan.

Down in the crowd, Key steadily edged toward the stage. He was not nervous. He felt ready. No one would see him coming. He crept closer, step by step. Not following the plan.

≪CHAPTER FORTY-THREE≫

Showdown

Scarlet tapped her earpiece. "Almost," she reported. "Get ready."

"Okay," Laurel said. She was responsible for sending up the signal. She waited.

"Come on, come on," Scarlet scolded herself. She pictured an MP tech staffer in a room somewhere receiving an intruder alert on his system. "Take that, lab boys," she whispered, her fingers flying over the keys. "So close. Come on . . . Got it!"

Scarlet tapped her ear again. "MP weapons neutralized. Good to go now!"

"Roger," said Key, from his spot in the crowd. He was well out of position by that point, but the girls could not tell from only his voice.

"Wilco," said Laurel. "Signaling now." She pulled a small device from her pocket and pressed the Play button.

Crack! BOOM!

The sound of huge thunder exploded from her fist.

"Whoa." Laurel reeled back. The sound was much more deafening than she expected. She pressed the button again.

Crack! BOOM!

The workers knew what to do. They broke ranks, bursting from their quiet rows. They leaped toward the MPs.

The MPs were not expecting an attack. As one, they looked toward the sky at the sound of thunder. As one, they reached for their sidearms as the crowd of workers surged toward them. As one, they faltered as the little red lights on their weapons failed to turn green at their touch.

It was a melee. Hand-to-hand combat broke out between workers and MPs all across the square. The workers attempted to subdue the MPs and get up onstage to reach Crown and Mallet.

MPs pressed in to enclose the area where the thunderclap originated. But Laurel was long gone. She slipped through the crowd and made her way back to the rooftop. *You can get out of anywhere if you're small.*

Mallet jumped down from the stage to help fight off the first wave of workers that approached the platform. She was a formidable fighter, even without a weapon.

Crown remained trapped on the stage, unable to get down the stairs due to the fighting. He stood there, next to the chained-up Loxleys.

Lucille Loxley worked her tongue until the gag pushed loose. "You can kill us, but the movement will only grow stronger," she shouted. "You cannot kill the rebellion."

Crown flinched at the sound of her voice, but he did not attempt to replace her gag. Such work was clearly beneath him. He watched Mallet beating down workers who tried to approach the stage. She and the MPs had his back. He didn't need to worry.

$$\gg\!\!\!\longrightarrow$$

Key moved closer to the stage, eyeing Crown all the while. He looked for a break in the crowd. When he found one, he leaped forward. He mounted the stage, carrying a real gun in his hand. An old-style gun, no handprint needed.

He fired into the air. The whole crowd paused in surprise. All the guns were supposed to be inactive.

"What are you doing?" Robyn held her earpiece as she spoke. She remained tucked at the center of the crowd, surrounded by workers who would fight to keep her safe.

Key didn't answer. He advanced across the stage. "I've been waiting for this moment all my life," he said to Crown. "You killed my mother. You threw me away, but I didn't die. And now you will."

≪CHAPTER FORTY-FOUR≫

Sacrifice

Marissa Mallet registered two things at once: A gun, trained on Ignomus Crown, and a familiar-looking boy standing behind it.

Instinct took over.

Mallet leaped back onto the stage and stood between Crown and the threat. The boy flinched as she moved between him and his target.

In the moment, it felt only natural. Seconds later, her body flooded with a disturbing mix of fear and shame.

You threw me away. The boy's words echoed through her.

Ignomus had cast her aside, too. Who was this boy, and why was he able to speak the truth of her heart so deeply?

"Get out of my way," he said.

"You can't win," Mallet told him quietly. "You are surrounded."

The boy stood trembling before her, but his gun arm remained distressingly firm. She could take him down with a lunge. She just might take a bullet in the process.

Mallet hesitated.

She was prepared to lay down her life for Ignomus Crown. It was her job. And yet, just as fully, she knew he didn't deserve her sacrifice.

"Foolish boy," Crown muttered. "You'll never get to me." His voice, so full of certainty, of cruelty, hit her harder than a bullet ever could. Her heart cracked. She could go down in a bloody heap, dying to defend him, and he wouldn't think anything of it at all. Her throat clogged and her vision blurred.

$$\ggg\!\!\longrightarrow$$

"Step aside," Key said, his gun now trained on Mallet. "It's Crown I want." He licked his lips nervously. This wasn't going as planned. He hadn't counted on the sheriff stepping in.

He had only three bullets. He'd already fired one, which now seemed reckless.

It was supposed to go quickly. Climb the stairs. Point the gun. Shoot.

He'd planned it in his head. Over and over. All night. And for months before that. Years, maybe.

But the trigger was taut. Pulling it into the air had shaken him. His arm felt weak, though his heart continued to scream for justice. For an end to all of this pain.

The girls were shouting into his earpiece. A cacophony. It blurred into static. There was his finger, not moving. His heart, bursting out of his body. And Crown, smiling through the horror before him.

"Did you ever wonder—" Key tried to speak, but his voice caught in some place invisible.

A blur of thoughts won his mind then. What it might have been like to live a different kind of life. To be loved from the beginning. To have everything, to live in a castle on a hill.

What it might have been like to look at the man across the stage and feel affection instead of rage. To feel taken in, instead of thrown out.

What if everything had been different?

"You can't win," the sheriff was saying. But it wasn't her words that mattered. It was those bitter, cold eyes. The flash of recognition that didn't fade into . . .

Key's resolve returned. "Step aside," he repeated.

To his amazement, the sheriff did.

Crown's certainty faltered as his shield disappeared. His eyes flicked, shocked, toward Mallet, then trained back on Key.

"You're the child?" Crown said. "You survived?"

Everything was his finger on the trigger. There was nothing else. There was no seeing himself in this cruel man's eyes. No hope of being seen.

Key nodded. "Did you ever think about what would happen if I lived? If I ever found out who I really was?"

He was met with silence. Cold, bitter eyes. No sudden joy. No open arms. No change at all.

The most secret hope of his heart. Denied.

Key tightened his trigger finger. There was no going back.

>>>——→

Robyn drifted closer to the stage. What had gotten into Key? Now she saw his anger and threats from last night in a new light. He hadn't been blowing off steam, or theorizing. He had wanted to literally kill Crown. Why?

You threw me away, he said. His voice trembled through the words, so he must have felt them deeply. But Crown cast everyone aside. What made Key's situation so different?

"You killed my mother," Key said. Robyn had long suspected that Key had lost his family in tragic circumstances. Was Crown directly to blame? That came as no surprise to Robyn.

Plenty of things about this moment did surprise her, though:

Key with a gun. A working gun.

The faltering of the fights around the square as everyone turned to look at the stage.

The surge of desperate hope in her own heart. The depth of her own desire to see Crown ended, right before her eyes.

And the sheriff. She faced off with Key, obviously poised to take him down. To protect Crown with her own body. But then something happened. For a moment, the sheriff's resolve to protect the governor appeared to waver. Mallet's gaze grew softer, less certain.

Most surprising of all, the sheriff stepped aside.

On the stage, Key held the gun on Crown.

The pause stretched out for an eternity.

From the side angle, Mallet dove for Key, knocking him to the floor. Her hand cupped his, as they went down, wrestling for control. The gun fell from Key's hand. It slid across the stage. The governor bent and picked it up.

Crown took the gun in his hand with a triumphant smile. He fired it in the air and then pointed it immediately at Robyn's parents. "We're here for an execution, after all."

⫷CHAPTER FORTY-FIVE⫸

Surrender

Crown pointed the gun at Robyn's father. "End this, or I'll end them!"

Sacrifice. The word echoed in Robyn's head. She had known it might come to this. She had known all along she might have to give them up for the good of the cause. She steeled herself.

"Going once . . . ," Crown shouted.

Sacrifice. Her parents wanted it this way. They preferred it this way. They would gladly give their lives to spare hers, and to mobilize a movement. *Gladly?* No. They would not be glad to die, of course. But glad to have lived and died with such meaning.

"Going twice . . . ,"

Sacrifice. It meant something different to her now. It meant something more than giving up the things she loved. It meant giving of herself.

"Going three times . . . Last chance . . ." Crown drew out the finale, slowly raising the gun to Robert's head.

Crown sighed. "Very well, then." He pressed the gun harder against Robert's temple. Her father closed his eyes.

"STOP!" Robyn screamed into the digital megaphone. "I'm coming. I'm coming."

There was no other way. No chance she could stand by and watch her parents killed.

Sacrifice.

If nothing else, Sherwood would know that the girl they called Robyn Hoodlum could not let another person die in her place. That would have to be enough. It was all she had left to give.

Robyn charged toward the stage. The voices in her head clamored for attention, as her friends all shouted variations of "No, don't do it!"

"*Shh,*" Robyn said. She rolled up onto the stage, forgoing the stairs.

Then it was just Key's voice in her ear. Telling her all she needed to know.

"No, baby, no," her mother cried.

"I can't, Mom," Robyn answered, never taking her eyes off Crown. "I can't let him kill you."

Crown's face softened into his warped version of a smile. "I knew it."

"You think you're ahead of me?" Robyn told him. "You aren't."

"Guess again, hoodlum," Crown answered.

"How many bullets do you think are left in that gun?" Robyn said. "I'll give you a hint."

Crown did not lower the weapon, but his eyes shifted left to right. "You think I'm a fool?" he said. "I lower this gun and you take me? Never going to happen." He pivoted, turning the gun on Robyn instead of her father.

Robyn shrugged. "I'm saying, I know the person who loaded it. And I know there are not as many bullets in it as you think."

One bullet, to be precise. Key had just told her.

"I'm sorry, Robyn," Key whispered. "It was for him. I meant them for him." At the other corner of the stage, Mallet held Key, strapping cuffs on him as they watched the scene unfold.

Crown looked nervous. "There are plenty of bullets," he said. "Or you wouldn't be standing there looking so scared."

"I think you're the one who should be scared," Robyn answered. "The people have spoken, and we've voted you out!"

A cheer rang up from the crowd. But no one actually moved. Crown still had the gun trained on Robyn.

"The people have spoken," Robyn cried again. She held the wooden arrow aloft. "You can shoot me now," she told Crown. "You can cut me down in front of all these people. Claim the power that you so deeply desire. But you won't make it off this stage. You won't make it back to your car."

Crown's eyes shifted. The MP guns were still inactive, thanks to Scarlet. They would have to defend him hand-to-hand if the crowd surged forward again. And they no doubt would come for him the moment the hoodlum was dead.

Robyn flicked the switch that silenced the megaphone. "Or, you can be smart. Take me." She stepped closer to him. She held out her arms. "I'm turning myself in."

$$\gg\!\!\!\longrightarrow$$

Merryan watched helplessly from within the car as Robyn surrendered to her uncle.

"Without me, you'll be trapped in Sherwood," Robyn told Crown. "They'll let you go if I'm your prisoner. No one wants me harmed."

Robyn placed her hands behind her head. From there she could still reach her earpiece.

High on the rooftop, Laurel leaned excitedly toward Scarlet. Robyn, too, heard what she whispered through their intercom.

"Mark this moment," Crown announced to the square. "The hoodlum's unconditional surrender."

Unconditional?

"Not exactly," Robyn shouted. "The deal was my parents go free."

Crown smiled his oiliest smile. "The deal was, your parents live. Step toward me now."

"Not until you release them! You cannot go back on your word."

Crown edged closer to Robyn, the gun very much the object of focus. "You have a lot to learn about effective negotiations, my dear."

He was right, and she knew it. She'd walked into his trap, and hope now was slim.

"Get him to the car," Scarlet said into Robyn's ear. "And I'll see what I can do."

"Very well," Robyn said. "I've surrendered."

"Walk," he ordered her. She marched slowly toward him.

Robyn's mother wept quiet tears as she passed. "Be strong, baby, we love you."

"We love you," her father echoed. It had been months since she'd seen him. He appeared gaunt and scruffy, with chapped lips and thick puffs of hair poking up from his head. "We're proud of you."

"I love you both, too," Robyn answered. It was all she could do not to run over and embrace them. Crown would destroy her as soon as he got her away from the crowd. Her parents would be returned to prison. She had failed.

Behind her head, she held the Arrow of Truth in one hand. Tucker's writing flashed through her mind, in one clear piece.

The shrines have burned. You want to have faith because your father has faith. But the world is not black and white. The answers aren't written in curtains or texts. It's you, in the world, who finds the answers.

Out of nowhere, Robyn understood this scribbled message. The moon lore was meant to be a guide, a comfort. She could cling to her arrow all she wanted. There were no easy answers.

No miracle was coming. She was entirely on her own.

≺CHAPTER FORTY-SIX≻

The Arrow of Truth

The lonely feeling pierced her suddenly, the way an Arrow of Truth actually might. Then the slow, helpless ache stretched out for a long minute after that. Robyn stood perfectly still at the center of the stage, with Crown's gun trained on her.

The mass crowd movement had trapped him. A few minutes ago he had been unable to leave the stage to get to his car, but with Robyn as hostage, everything changed.

"It's okay. Let him through," Robyn said quietly. The crowd parted. Not for Crown, but for her.

The governor inched Robyn toward the motorcade. He kept the gun trained on her. They moved as one toward the car. "The car doors," Laurel blurted again, excitedly. "They're computerized!"

"I heard you," Scarlet said. But from somewhere within the MP headquarters, Mallet's lab techs were still fighting back against Scarlet's gun-hacking efforts.

"Well?" Robyn whispered. "We're almost there."

"I'm in, but I can't control both systems at once," Scarlet cried. "It's either the guns or the car doors. I have to let go of one."

"You can do it," Robyn answered. "It's not for much longer." The workers were making their way through Crown's perimeter of security.

"No, I literally can't," Scarlet said. "It's two separate systems."

They had almost reached the vehicle. Crown pivoted, keeping the gun trained on Robyn until he had Robyn pressed right up against the door of his vehicle.

Through the glass, Merryan stared horrified at the sight of her friend in trouble. She reached for the door handle, but Robyn shook her head quickly. "No!" she mouthed. Merryan pulled her hand back.

Crown pivoted until his back was against the door. He could reach behind him, open the door, and pull Robyn inside along with him. By keeping her between him and the crowd, he would never be exposed to danger.

"Robyn?" Scarlet asked. "What do you want me to do?"

"Get Crown," Key shouted from the stage. "Whatever it takes."

"We can get Crown this way," Scarlet confirmed. "But once the guns are active, we'll lose a lot of others in the process."

Robyn considered the problem. Once Crown was in the protected vehicle, he was as good as safe. They'd lose the best chance they ever had to take him down.

The doors, or the guns? Risk losing Crown, or risk that all the MPs might start firing at will.

Robyn's gaze landed on the stage. Sheriff Mallet stood completely still, watching the scene unfold.

To succeed in this journey you will be required to trust. Eveline's words floated back to her. She gripped the arrow in her fist so tightly it practically vibrated.

Trust Mallet?

Wasn't that a bridge too far? Mallet could not be trusted.

But then again, hadn't Robyn thought that about everyone at one point? And here they were, working together. She trusted Scarlet to keep the car doors locked. She trusted Key when he said they were dealing with one bullet. She had trusted Merryan's warning that Crown was coming, and all the advice Jeb had given them about the MPs. She trusted Laurel implicitly.

The Arrow of Truth, right now, was trust. And community. The realization shocked Robyn to the core. Here and now, she was the opposite of alone.

But . . . to trust Mallet?

The world is not black and white . . .

Robyn could trust her own instincts. Trust the glimmer she'd seen in Mallet's eye. Trust that her moving aside for Key was only the first step. Trust that with Robyn's pendant around her neck, the sheriff would be forced to see more clearly. Trust the words that were rising up in her now, a gift from Tucker's dissertation:

The answers aren't written in curtains or texts. It's you, in the world, who finds the answers.

"Okay, let us in the car," Crown ordered, reaching for the door handle. The driver poked at his PalmTab to unlatch the doors.

Sacrifice.

"Doors!" Robyn shouted. The worst that could happen, whether they were inside the car or out, was that Crown would shoot her. She looked up at the stage, to her parents. They had been willing to give up everything. So was she. Robyn would not let them, or Sherwood down.

Scarlet pounded the keyboard. "You sure?"

Crown tugged at the car door handle, but the metal didn't budge. He tugged again. "What are you doing?" he demanded of Robyn. "You surrendered."

"I take it back," Robyn told him. "Neither of us is going anywhere."

Crown's grip around her shoulders tightened. "You just signed your death warrant," he whispered.

"So be it. Release the MP guns," Robyn ordered Scarlet. "Don't let Crown back in the car."

Crown smiled complacently. The MPs would protect him. He was as good as safe.

Maybe not, Robyn thought.

"Sheriff Marissa Mallet!" Robyn's voice rang out across the square. "You wear the Pendant of Power, blessed by the moon and the sun. You are a child of Shadows and Light. The people of Sherwood place their trust in you."

Mallet's hand flitted to the pendant resting on her chest. A wave of hope flooded Robyn.

Around the square, the red lights on the MPs guns flipped to green.

"What are your orders?" Robyn shouted. "When you look upon the faces of this crowd, do you see any enemies?"

The hoodlum's courage had captured the hearts of the crowd, and Mallet's along with them. With a wave of her hand, she could make this fight much worse for Robyn and her friends.

And yet.

The pendant against her chest promised power. But it also commanded respect.

How was it that this scrawny rebel child and her haughty words could make the sheriff of Sherwood believe in something so deep?

The hoodlum Robyn had cast a spell on the people of Sherwood. To cut her down now, in front of this crowd, would mean full-scale, all-out rebellion. MPs would fall like dominoes. As if it was written.

Mallet punched her PalmTab. She ordered her tech guys to keep the MP guns turned off, leaving Crown exposed. The workers closed in on him.

The gun Crown held at Robyn meant nothing now, and he knew it. One bullet was not enough. The crowd of workers would ultimately destroy him.

"Let me in," Crown screamed, pounding on the door of the car. "Let me in!"

Merryan Crown made no move to open the door for her uncle. Even if she could have.

Crown's driver looked urgently at his PalmTab. The doors would not open. Still, he valiantly typed and pecked until—*click*.

"No!" Scarlet shouted from the rooftop.

The car door locks snapped open. Crown heard the click and scrambled for the door handle. He grasped it and tugged, but the door still failed to open.

He stared through the glass, shocked to see Merryan holding the lock button in place with her own hands. "Merryan!" he shouted. "Let me in."

Tears streamed down Merryan's pale cheeks. "I'm sorry, uncle. I'm sorry." Through the window she met Robyn's eye. The look they shared said everything.

$$\ggg\!\!\longrightarrow$$

Crown remained trapped against his car, while everyone stood and watched him slowly unravel. The MPs stood in a protective circle around his car, but made no moves to attack the workers.

The gun in Crown's hand was still an object of concern, especially to Robyn, as it was still pointed at her neck.

"I will kill her," Crown informed everyone. "Stay back."

Mallet approached them. "Governor," she said. "Let the girl go. Let me take her into custody."

Robyn did not especially like the sound of that, either.

"Do not test me, Marissa. You have no idea what I'm capable of." There was a sadness to his voice, buried within its chill.

He would kill her. Of this, Robyn had no doubt. But he hadn't killed her yet.

The tip of the gun rested at the base of her neck. Her fingers, still resting behind her head, were almost close enough . . .

Robyn spun around and kneed Crown in the groin. She leaned hard to the side, in case he fired, then skidded out from under his arm as he bent forward in pain. She grasped the gun from his loosened grip and streaked away.

She clambered over the hood of the car, eager to put space between herself and Crown. She tugged open the driver's side door. "Get out," she said. The gun in her hand communicated her message loud and clear, although she hadn't even pointed it at the driver. He scrambled out of the car and away.

Robyn jumped into the driver's seat, and Scarlet locked her safely inside. She set the gun on the passenger seat, then turned and looked over the front seat divide. "Hi."

"Hi," Merryan answered. "Wanna get me outta here?"

Robyn laughed shakily. She stretched her hand through the opening and Merryan grasped it.

"I'm alive," Robyn mused. "I wasn't sure I was going to be."

The girls held hands and watched through the glass as Mallet grasped the moaning Crown by the shoulders and stood him upright.

"Time was, you'd have taken that bullet for me," Crown said to her.

"Time was," Mallet agreed. She wrenched Crown's hands behind his back and clasped cuffs on his wrists. "Ignomus Crown, you're under arrest for treason and acts against the elected government."

The moon lore pendant swung freely, tapping against her suit buttons. As she took Crown into custody, the whole crowd cheered.

⊰CHAPTER FORTY-SEVEN⊱

Power to the People

Sheriff Mallet briskly took command of the situation. First she took Crown into her own car, detaining him behind her own set of electronic locks.

Next, Mallet ordered the Loxleys to be released from their chains. Robyn's parents immediately embraced, supporting each other as they moved to the front of the stage. Meanwhile, Robyn was attempting a slow, awkward getaway.

Mallet came down and knocked on the car window. "Come out," she said.

Robyn shook her head. "And get arrested? No, thanks." She attempted to steer the car out of the motorcade, but the crowd made maneuvering difficult.

"It's okay," Mallet told her. "The crowd needs to see you back up here."

"How do I know she won't take me straight into custody?" Robyn muttered.

"How did you know she would order the MPs to stand down?" Merryan asked.

Point taken.

Robyn stepped out of the car. She accompanied Sheriff Mallet to the stage. The sheriff wore Robyn's own pendant, which now hung in broad view for all to see.

"I will release the Loxleys as a show of good will toward the people of Sherwood," Mallet announced. "Robyn and I have a lot of work to do." She glanced at the girl. "Together."

They shook on it. Their hands were a similar shade of brown, and yet it felt like worlds colliding. Morning and night. Shadows and Light.

Robyn let go of the sheriff's hand and knelt beside her parents at the front of the stage. She hugged their weakened bodies, but their inner strength floated up and filled her.

"You're alive," she said. "I can't believe it."

"Oh, honey, you saved us," her mother whispered, holding her close.

"And you are in so much trouble, young lady," her father added. "Under no circumstances are you ever to deal with firearms ever again."

"Not even to save the world?" Robyn quipped.

"You *are* the world, to us," her mother told her.

"Nothing has changed about this workday," Mallet announced to the workers, many of whom lingered to witness the family's happy ending. "The showcase is over. Time to get on the job."

The crowd began to disperse.

The MPs who had been holding Key released him. It would have been all too easy to slip away into the crowd and disappear. He couldn't really explain why he didn't. Instead, he eased his way toward Robyn.

"You"—she said, narrowing her eyes at him—"have some explaining to do."

"I'm sorry," Key said. He sat down on the edge of the stage and rested his face in his hands.

Scarlet and Laurel came rushing up. "Let's get out of here, before Mallet changes her mind about arresting us," Scarlet said. "We gotta boogie."

"I think we're okay," Robyn said. "She was working for Crown all this time. She isn't like him."

Scarlet squinted over at Mallet. "You sure?"

Robyn also glanced toward the sheriff. The shrine key pendant caught her attention again. Funny, she didn't care much at all about the pendant at the moment. Now that she had her actual parents back, she didn't need a talisman to keep them close. Perhaps Mallet could use a little fire of her own.

Robyn shrugged. "I guess we're taking this one on faith."

$$\ggg\!\!\longrightarrow$$

The friends waited at the edge of the stage for their ride. Mr. and Mrs. Loxley had gone ahead in an ambulance to be checked out at Sherwood Health Clinic. It had been torture, watching her parents dragged away from her again, but this time Robyn knew they'd be reunited very soon.

Scarlet nudged Key. "Time to 'fess up, mister," she said. "You almost blew it for all of us."

Key hung his head. "I know. I'm sorry."

Robyn said gently, "So, I take it Crown is . . . your dad?"

Key nodded. "I always knew I was adopted. I had to be. My whole family is dark, and then there's me, looking like the marshmallow in a s'more."

"But you didn't know who your birth family was?"

Key shook his head. "My mom worked as a housekeeper in Crown's house, back before he was even police commissioner."

"He was police commissioner as long as I can remember," Merryan said.

"Apparently it all happened around the same time," Key said. His voice stayed very even, as if he was telling a story about someone else. "His wife—my birth mother—died giving birth to me. He—he didn't want to keep me after that."

"I'm sorry," Robyn whispered.

"He tried to smother me." Key's voice remained flat. "But he didn't finish the job. He handed the baby to his housekeeper to dispose of, thinking I was dead."

"Oh, for the moon," Laurel said. "He's so horrible."

"I didn't die," Key continued. "But no one knew except my mother. She ran, and never returned. She knew he'd kill me if she took me back, and she thought he might eventually kill her, too, for knowing what he'd done."

"She was probably right about that," Robyn said. "Crown would do anything to preserve his power."

"I only found out a couple of years ago. By accident. Mom had saved some items from my birth mom, things Crown threw out of the house along with me. She meant to give them to me when I was older. But when I found the box, I put the pieces together for myself."

"Sure," Scarlet said.

"My mom said it would have been a terrible life, if he had raised me," Key added. "She thought he would have resented me forever. He loved her so much, my mom said. Losing her was part of what turned him evil." Key looked to Robyn, a question in his eyes.

"She was probably right about that, too," Robyn agreed. He really wanted to believe it, she could tell.

They stood together in silence for a moment.

"So . . . that means . . . you're the baby?" Merryan exclaimed. "My dead cousin?"

"Not so dead, as it turns out," Key said dryly.

"But . . . so . . . you're my cousin." Merryan and Key looked at each other. Then she jumped up and tackled him in a giant hug. He surrendered with good-natured surprise.

"Well, that was predictable," Robyn said.

Key tapped on Merryan's back. "Let go," he choked out. "I wasn't smothered as a baby, and I don't want to be now."

Merryan let him go. She turned around to face Robyn, planting her hands on her hips. "Exactly what was predictable about that?"

Robyn smirked. "You like to hug people."

Merryan pretended to be annoyed, but she couldn't hold the expression. "That's true, I do," she declared, and leaped toward Robyn. Their arms went around each other, and while Merryan didn't hug her too insanely tight, Robyn felt the contact all up and down her body. It was snug and comfortable, a surprising feeling of home.

She pulled away when she felt an insistent finger tapping at her back.

"I knew how to help," Laurel chirped, still excited. "I told them how to do it."

"How did you know?" Robyn asked her.

Laurel smiled coyly. "When I jumped on that windshield, a little bug told me."

"You could've been squashed like a bug!" Robyn tousled her hair affectionately. "Crazy girl. You know you saved me, right? At least twice now."

Laurel hugged her. "We all saved each other, you mean. That's how it goes around Sherwood now."

Robyn looked at her friends, knowing Laurel was right. They needed everyone in order to succeed at this effort. All the Elements. Scarlet's hacking skills. Laurel's tip about the car locks. Merryan's betrayal of her uncle. Jeb's earpieces and insider MP knowledge. Tucker's dissertation writings. Even Key's rash threat against Crown had made possible this outcome.

It wasn't just Robyn—not just one person, one fire, one hero who saved the day. It was all of them together. And it felt wonderful.

≪CHAPTER FORTY-EIGHT≫

Home at Last

The members of the Crescendo gathered at Nessa Croft's home at the edge of Sherwood Heights. The place was a bit dusty, as she had been on the run and unable to return home in recent months. But everyone was enthusiastic about helping her get the place into shape. Now, they sat around the living room, discussing the events of the day.

"With Mallet in charge of security, things will stay tight for a while," Nessa predicted.

"It's not ideal," Chazz agreed. "But those MPs sure leap when she says how high."

"Yes, we need her," Lucille Loxley said. "She's turning out to be a reasonable woman, now that she's not answering to that maniac Crown."

"Officially, all the political prisoners have been released," Robert Loxley reported. He hung up the phone. "We're sending cars to pick them up and bring them here."

"Everybody? Here?" Nessa said, glancing around. It was a decent-sized home for one person, but it was already cramped with Crescendo workers.

"We'd like to make sure everyone is doing all right before we send them on to their own homes." Robert cringed. "That is, those that aren't going straight to the hospital."

"Send a car for Tucker!" Robyn cried. She was eager to see him. It would be a miracle, seeing all the Elements gathered together once again. In person.

It was amazing how far they'd come in the space of a couple of days.

Jeb no longer had to feel guilty for serving as an MP. With Crown out of power, Sherwood could be policed fairly again.

Scarlet would surely go on challenging the technological infrastructure of the whole city, hopefully making a stronger and safer Sherwood for them all. She sat on the floor even now, tapping away at her screens.

Laurel was ready to take the world by storm. She was practically climbing the walls in her excitement. Nessa handed her a damp cloth and set her to dusting.

Merryan was seated next to Robyn on the couch. Merryan, who . . . well, she had given up one family. She deserved to find another. Robyn took her hand and held it. "You were the bravest of all of us," she said.

Merryan ducked her head. Her bobbed hair curtained across her face. "I think it was the right thing."

"It totally was." Robyn was certain. But she also knew how hard it must have been. Merryan had achieved what even she, the so-called savior of Sherwood, had not been able to do: to give up her loved ones for the cause.

Sacrifice. That was the theme of the day, for certain. "I don't know where I'm going to go," Merryan said in a small voice.

Robyn squeezed her hand. "You're going to stay right here with me."

The girls embraced. Merryan rested her cheek on Robyn's shoulder as they watched the rest of the room.

Key stood leaning against the wall. He was lucky Mallet had let him go along with the others, Robyn knew. And she knew something else, too: Key might be rash, but he was not a killer. When push came to shove he could not take the life of the father he hated. She could have told him that long before he stormed the stage, if he'd asked her.

"Tucker's on his way," Robert reported. "He'll be here soon."

Tucker, Robyn hoped, would finish his dissertation. His words would remind everyone that the moon lore was important history—one that could inspire or guide people—but that it was just that . . . history.

Robyn was sure she would still look up at the moon, seeking answers. She would smile every time a painted arrow crossed into her vision. She might even try to crack the curtain messages, for old times' sake. But it wouldn't be because she thought those ancient words would magically solve her problems.

It had never been magic, she understood now. It had always been clues. It urged her to rely on friends, when all she knew was how to be alone.

It urged her to look for the strength in herself, believing it was written. Could she have become Robyn Hoodlum without that special helping of faith? She doubted it.

Robyn knew now that the true power of the moon lore was hers, from someplace inside. A place too deep and too hidden to see in the light of a perfect day. A place that only showed itself under the shadow of struggle.

"Wonderful. When they get here, we can all go home," Lucille Loxley said.

Robyn's ears perked to that. "Home?" she echoed. "What do you mean? Aren't we here?" For some reason she'd thought they'd be staying with Nessa for a while.

Her parents both looked at her. "We'll be going back to Loxley Manor shortly, of course," her mother said.

"But—no," Robyn cried. "We can't." Her throat choked up and her eyes overflowed. Returning to Castle District meant things would go back to how they used to be. The thought caused her to burst into tears.

Merryan hugged Robyn harder. She was crying, too. "It'll be okay," she said.

"How? How will it?" Robyn cried. Scarlet paused her typing and looked up. She moved her foot, nudging Robyn's toes with hers.

Key sat down on the sofa next to her. "Hey," he said. "We won, remember?"

A very bouncy Laurel scampered closer, perching on the back of the sofa, close to Robyn. "Yeah, we won," she echoed.

Robyn struggled to hold back her sobs. It didn't make sense to cry now, when everything was fine. The worst was over.

But the idea of heading back to Castle District struck her hard. Loxley Manor was forever tainted by the things that had happened there. Her memory of the Night of Shadows was strong. Would she ever be able to walk into that kitchen and not remember seeing her father's blood on the floor? And, that whole past life was tainted by the knowledge that living there had separated Robyn and her father from the community that was rightfully theirs. Sherwood.

"You know, everything isn't magically fixed because Crown is removed," Robert said. "There's a lot more work to be done to put Nott City back together the way it should be."

"I know." Robyn sniffled. "But can't we do it from here, in Sherwood?"

Robert looked thoughtful. "I don't know. Our work is with Parliament, and that's in Castle District."

"You want to stay in Sherwood?" her mother asked, with surprise.

"I fit here," Robyn told them. "I found friends here." They clustered around her now, all in their own way trying to attend to her sudden sadness.

"We'll think about it," her father said.

Robyn threw her arms around Key and Laurel, smashing Merryan close in the process. She nudged Scarlet's foot back with her own. "It's just that—I'm not the only one who needs a good place to live."

Mrs. Loxley looked at her husband. "Well, they did save our lives."

He nodded thoughtfully. "We always intended to have a bigger family."

Robyn held her breath. Her parents studied the faces of her daughter's friends. Laurel. Key. Scarlet. Merryan. The thought of turning them out into the cold . . . no. They could never.

"We can't abandon Loxley Manor," Mrs. Loxley said. "It's a family legacy."

Robert shrugged. "We wouldn't be abandoning it. We'd be embracing a different family legacy."

"In Sherwood!" Robyn exclaimed.

"We can get you a good deal on a brownstone," Key suggested. "We have the technology."

Scarlet grinned impishly. "Sure. You are the great hero of Sherwood, after all. I can peek into the For Sale listings and find you something great."

Robyn shook her head. "Not 'you,'" she corrected them. "Us."

$$\ggg\!\longrightarrow$$

Robyn and her friends grabbed warm chocolate chip cookies off straight off the cooling rack. Mrs. Loxley and Nessa had been busy cooking meals and treats for everyone all afternoon.

"We're going out," Robyn reported. "It's way too crowded in here." Now that the freed people had arrived, the house was a jubilant mess of recuperation and celebration, and they were all feeling underfoot.

"Be back by sunset," Mrs. Loxley said. "I know you kids are used to running around unsupervised, but I'm here now. Dinner's at seven." She gave them a stern look, which slowly faded into a smile.

"Sure, Mom." Robyn ran across the kitchen and hugged her. "We'll be hungry. We promise."

"Thank you, Mrs. Loxley," Merryan said politely, raising her cookie.

"Let's go," Laurel said. "First things first. Toothbrush sheets!"

Key rolled his eyes. "That is not even remotely our first stop."

"Why not?" Laurel protested as she slid on her shoes in the front hallway.

"Too mundane," Scarlet agreed.

Laurel was indignant. "There is nothing mundane about toothbrushes," she declared.

"Oh, for—" Scarlet giggled as she bumped Laurel's shoulder. "There's so much better trouble we can cause. You need to have a greater vision. Clearly, we have a lot of work to do."

Robyn and her friends ran out the door, laughing. "Sherwood hasn't seen the last of Robyn Hoodlum!"

Acknowledgments

I remain deeply grateful to my family and the many friends who support, uplift, comfort, and inspire me as I work. Special thanks to Will, Alice, Liam, and Iris for keeping me well fed when the deadlines were looming. Also, thanks to Nicole Valentine, Emily Kokie, Sarah Badavas, Cynthia Leitich Smith, Kerry Land, and Michelle Humphrey for their support, as well as all of my colleagues at Vermont College of Fine Arts. Finally, thanks to my agent, Ginger Knowlton, my editor, Mary Kate Castellani, and the entire team at Bloomsbury, who combine their creative talents to transform each book from an idea to a reality.